Mills & Boon
Best Seller Romance

A chance to read and collect some of the best-loved novels from Mills & Boon—the world's largest publisher of romantic fiction.

Every month, six titles by favourite Mills & Boon authors will be re-published in the *Best Seller Romance* series.

A list of other titles in the *Best Seller Romance* series can be found at the end of this book.

Violet Winspear

THE BURNING SANDS

MILLS & BOON LIMITED
LONDON · TORONTO

First published 1976
Australian copyright 1983
Philippine copyright 1983
This edition 1983

© Violet Winspear 1976

ISBN 0 263 74187 7

Set in 10 on 11 pt. Garamond
02–0183

Made and printed in Great Britain by
Richard Clay (The Chaucer Press) Ltd,
Bungay, Suffolk

CHAPTER ONE

THE uncertain sunlight of an autumn day slanted down on the flame-red hair of a girl who sat in a basket chair on a balcony, scanning idly the pages of a magazine whose glossy cover was adorned by a Tudor house set among oak trees.

All at once Sarah's attention was no longer idle and she was gazing at a paragraph as if it mesmerised her. It was quaintly worded, even slightly equivocal in a column of print otherwise devoted to the sale of secondhand fur coats, wigs made from natural hair, and copper warming-pans:

> Young woman of British birth required to live abroad in the capacity of companion, in the household of a gentleman of means.

Sarah blinked, for the advertisement was like a relic out of the Victorian era, when impoverished young women sailed out to foreign places to provide companionship for the wives and daughters of planters or men in the colonial service.

But this was the jet age, and long gone were the days when girls like Jane Eyre travelled from orphan homes to dwell in establishments where the mistress might be a tartar and the master a tyrant. Nowadays young women did every sort of job but the one stated in this riveting advertisement. Sarah decided that it had to be some kind of a hoax . . . except that the magazine in which it was placed was hardly the sort that went in for practical jokes at the expense of its readers.

A young woman was required to live abroad, but it didn't state where. Any interested party was to write to a

5

box number, care of the magazine staff at their office in Bride Lane in London.

The green eyes of Sarah Innocence became reflective as she considered this outmoded appeal for a female companion. The bait for the hook was obviously that bit about the household being that of a gentleman of means, and there had to be a catch somewhere. Any fool of a girl who answered such an advertisement had to be desperate for a job, or too recklessly unhappy to care what became of her when she arrived at this foreign household.

The sun was fading from the sky when the balcony door opened and a woman in blue and white came out to Sarah. "Time for you to come in, Miss Innocence." She spoke in the unfailingly cheerful tones of the well-trained nurse at a high-priced clinic. "We don't want you taking a chill on top of everything else, now do we?"

That indulgent 'we' always amused Sarah, as if the nurse were talking to a child instead of a female adult of twenty-four years who had gone through a physical and emotional crisis which had left her unhappy and disillusioned. Life had been so good to her, but now she was wide awake to the reality of being a girl without a job, whose financial position had become very shaky indeed. After she paid her bills at the Regency Clinic she would be almost broke and would have to sell all the nice things at her flat, not to mention most of the contents of her wardrobe, in order to survive until some kind of an occupation presented itself.

Sarah rose from the basket chair and in her quilted robe followed the nurse into her private room. The flowers on the bedside table were starting to wilt, and the shadows of evening were collecting in the corners of this room in which she had suffered quite a lot of physical and mental pain in the past few weeks.

"What are you thinking of doing when you leave us?" the nurse asked, lifting one of the rounded jars from the dressing-table and sniffing at its fragrant contents.

"Oh — I thought of going abroad to work."

The nurse turned and gave Sarah a surprised look. In answer to her stare she received a slightly cynical smile — oh yes, they all knew that Sarah was finished as a model, for this was the nurse who had found her crying after the doctor had left. She was also the one who had picked up Peter's ring from off the floor, where Sarah had flung it. A jade set in pearls, to match her eyes and skin he had said, swearing that he loved her — the way she smiled and moved and made such a success of being a top flight model.

The twist of the knife in the wound was that Sarah had been thrown from the horse while at Peter's country house. Tossed against a tree and severely injured, to emerge several operations later with a left foot that would never assist her as before in that graceful saunter which was so essential to the girl who modelled clothes for a living! A limping model was about as popular as a bee at a barbecue!

"Don't look so surprised," she said. "Being a model, or being the wife of the Honourable Peter Johnson, aren't the only occupations in the world. Miss Innocence has become redundant in those fields, but she can branch out elsewhere, can't she? The market is wide open, nurse. I'm selling what I have to sell — myself!"

"Oh dear —" The nurse pressed a hand to her mouth. "I do hope you aren't going to do something foolish with your life, not after we went to such lengths to save it for you. Come, you're having me on, aren't you?"

"I was never more serious." Sarah sat on the foot of her bed and considered her slim left leg which was still firmly taped at the ankle. "I've been modelling for six years and in that time I earned good money, and I spent it as I made it. Those years have been hard work but fun, but now the party's over and I'm almost flat broke. I have to do something to live, so I'm going to grab at a chance that might take me as far away from England as I can get.

Broken bones mend, but hearts get kind of bitter, especially in a business where like a singer or an actress you're only as good as your last performance. It wouldn't have mattered about my limp if –"

She broke off and her lips twisted. Peter Jameson was out of her life and she didn't really want him back, not a man who hadn't the charity to stand by her. It was the slim, faultless body he had wanted, and now it was damaged he threw her aside like a broken doll.

Sarah's eyes glinted like green gems in her finely boned face, its contours both delicate and enduring, so that as a model she had been able to look exactly as the photographer demanded – a Garbo-like creature in sable skins, or a wet-skinned gamine running free and innocent on a spumy beach.

To hell with Peter and his like! His kind of love wasn't worth a second thought, and from this moment onward she vowed to keep her heart to herself, and to keep emotion out of any arrangement she made with a man.

Young British woman required to become a companion in a rich man's house, if the advertisement was to be believed. A gentleman of means resident in a foreign climate, and right now she'd give anything to climb aboard a jet plane and be carried miles away from the memory of a bolting horse, hours of pain in a sickroom, and the prospect of seeing another girl take her place in the modelling limelight. It wasn't envy, but the bitter pill of having worked so tirelessly only to lose it all on the toss of a horse.

Well, she didn't intend to stay around in order to collect sympathy and the regrets of the agencies that she was no longer in demand to saunter in silk and to thresh her long legs in the surf, the desirable object that sold anything from high-priced scent to the very latest in Gucci shoes.

Better by far to get away, but she hadn't the money to take her further than a bedsitter somewhere in a shabby part of London. She could no longer afford the rent of her tower flat, and she didn't fancy going back into a machine-shop to sew clothes until her eyes blurred and her shoulders cried out in silent agony.

She felt again as she had at the age of eighteen, when she had set out to conquer the modelling world. It had been a challenge and the Cockney blood in her veins thrived on a challenge.

Where, she wondered, in what part of the world lived this unknown gentleman who required a companion? Was it for his wife . . . an invalid, perhaps, who couldn't get about much and required someone to read to her and gossip about the goings on in England?

Well, there was plenty Sarah could talk about, and these people might not be put off by an ankle tendon which had been so severely injured that after the operations the surgeon had told her quite frankly that she would no longer walk with rhythm and poise – she would limp and it would show, but she was lucky not to have broken her neck.

The fiancé at whose country house she had been staying for the weekend, who had supplied her with that bad-tempered animal, was now so hateful to her that she had torn his photograph into fragments and scattered them from her balcony. Good riddance to romance, she thought. To hell with falling in love ever again!

"I had no idea you were thinking of going abroad to work, Miss Innocence." The nurse looked curious, and a little doubtful. "For the past few days you've seemed so anxious about the future and everything – is it something to do with modelling?"

"Not quite," said Sarah, with a reckless edge to her smile. "But if I land the job I feel sure I'll be able to cope with it. There's very little to keep me in England, and I don't think my gammy foot is going to stand in my way."

"I should hope not." The nurse ran admiring eyes over

the genuine red hair that cascaded about Sarah's shoulders, glinting in the glow of the bedside lamp. "I'm ever so glad that you've bucked up and haven't let your broken engagement to the Honourable Peter get you down."

"Honourable!" Sarah gave a cynical laugh. "Don't you mean dishonourable? Anyway, something like that teaches a girl a lesson and in future I shan't be a romantic idiot; I've had all that knocked out of me, with a vengeance."

"You mean you're not interested in marriage any more?" After all, even a nurse could be a romantic at heart and it had been a shame that this girl with her Garbo-like face should be jilted by a real live Honourable, especially one who was rather good-looking.

"I'm right off it," Sarah declared, with emphasis. "Men aren't interested in the person inside the body, and heaven help that body if it gets marked in any way. Men – they're like naughty little boys who class women among their playthings, and if any man comes near me with that attitude in mind – oh boy, will he get the sharp edge of my tongue!"

Sarah lay back against her pillows and curled an arm about her head, and her green eyes in the lamplight had almost a gleam of anticipation in them, as if she couldn't wait to cut to ribbons the first man who told her – as Peter had – that she was too attractive to be on her own with no one to take care of her. Scorn crept into her eyes, which slanted like green leaves against her white skin, the brown lashes tipped at the edges with a glint of flame.

"I don't want to go back to being a machinist in the East End," she said. "I couldn't take that after being a model. Yes, nurse, that's what I used to work at. I was reared by my grandmother, who put me to work in a machine-shop when I was sixteen, and I stuck it for just two years. In that time I grew rather willowy and I was frankly ambitious, and I knew that other Cockney girls had made the grade as models. Anyway, I struck lucky and met a photographer who said I had the right sort of bones for the job and for six years I was quite a success, and quite the rage at West End parties, where I met the Dishonourable Peter. He swore he adored me, do you know that? And I, like a gullible innocent, believed him. It was like the tale of Cinderella coming true, but the silver slipper doesn't fit my gammy foot and so the charming gentleman has gone off to – hell!"

Sarah lay silent a moment, gazing at the falling darkness beyond the windows of her room, then a sudden cold shiver ran through her as she contemplated the future. Dear old tartar Gran was dead and there was no one else who cared about her. It seemed that she had distant relatives in Scotland, but she had never met them, for they'd been on her father's side and he had died before her mother became ill going out to work in all weathers.

A sigh caught in Sarah's slim white throat. "So you took me for a society girl?" she murmured. "On the level, nurse?"

"Yes – I mean, look at the way you speak, and you've lovely manners, Miss Innocence." The blue and white figure leaned forward from the shadows and stared down at Sarah. "Is that your real name? It is unusual, if you don't mind me saying so."

"Yes, it really is my real name. The photographer who helped me to become a model thought I should keep it, for he said it had something. He was good to me – he and his wife Jane. They taught me how to speak like this, for at one time she was an actress and appeared in productions at Stratford-on-Avon. I was awfully grateful to both of them."

"Wouldn't they help you in your present trouble?" asked the nurse. "They sound such nice people, and you don't want to go doing anything you'll regret –"

"Like going abroad to earn my keep?" Sarah shrugged. "No, Jane and Harry have had troubles of their own with their son, and I won't inflict my woes on them. In any case, Harry couldn't help me any more with my modelling career – it's over and done with. It's a thing of the past and I have to face up to it."

"But you've lovely hair, Miss Innocence. What about shampoo adverts – couldn't you do those?"

"No, it wouldn't work for me. My appeal, if you care to call it that, lay in the way I walked and moved and thereby 'sold' the commodity that I wore. Now I'm lame, and I have to live with it. I either go back to machining all day in a stuffy factory, or I work for some man who won't mind that I am less than perfect."

"Oh, don't talk like that, Miss Innocence!" The nurse looked pained. "Not you, when you're so ladylike and nice, and we all admire you so much for the brave way you've taken your setback."

"Ugh, I'm not a nice lady, nurse. I'm a little cat with a sore foot and I'd like to scratch out Peter's eyes and howl on a wall for all I've lost. Believe me, I'm all burned up inside."

"Well, it's understandable, but things have a way of sorting themselves out, if you let them."

"I'd like to believe so." Sarah looked cynical. "But I've always found that if you want something then you have to make the effort and go after it. I want – escape, I suppose."

"And – and you think this job abroad can provide it?"

"I rather hope it can."

"Is it some sort of a foreigner you'll be working for?"

"I – really don't know." Sarah smiled slowly, but her eyes were a trifle bleak and wary. "It would be a turn-up for the book if he turned out to be foreign, wouldn't it?"

"Oh, miss, do think before you act. All sorts of funny things go on in these foreign places, and you'd be far safer to stay in England and get yourself a job. I'm sure with your looks and everything, you'd soon find something nice to do. What about an office in the city?"

"Yes, what about it?" Sarah grimaced and just couldn't picture herself in the role of the efficient secretary, jotting pad in hand, and so discreet on the telephone. "Being a model, nurse, doesn't equip a girl for a routine existence and I feel pretty certain that I wouldn't last a week cooped up in some office in the city. And being a shop assistant or a receptionist is ruled out by this foot of mine. I don't think it could take all that standing about behind a counter."

"Haven't you any money at all?" The nurse glanced from the expensive toiletries on the dressing-table, to the little jewelled watch that lay on the bedtable. "You must have earned good money – models get paid large fees, don't they? Not like nurses, I bet!"

"I've earned well and I've spent my portion, as it says in the good book. Now I must eat humble pie at the rich man's table, if I'm fortunate enough to be taken to his bosom. Oh, nurse, don't look at me like that! I told you I'm a determined girl from the Bow Bells area, not one of those elegant daddy's girls who stroll about Sloane Square in expensive silk head-scarves and blazers and work – if you can call it that – in charming little boutiques until a nice boy with a nice rich dad comes along."

Sarah set her jaw. "I have no option but to use what resources I have in order to live and not become a factory drudge like my poor mother. She couldn't afford to stay away from work even when she was ill, and coming home late from work one night she collapsed on the bus and was rushed to hospital with a bad dose of 'flu. She never recovered, and I'll do anything rather than follow in her shoes. Anything!"

The green eyes were reckless, and resolved. Women did it in the old days, didn't they? Went and worked for people they had never met! It was a bit of a risk, but it might be worth it, and she just wasn't going to be put off by the warnings of other people. From now on she would keep her plans to herself and not tell anyone that she was going to answer that advertisement for a companion. It was her business – hers and no one else's!

"Do be careful, Miss Innocence," urged the kindly nurse. "You've been through a traumatic experience and you're feeling low-spirited. Life always seems a bit of a dark pit when we're in trouble."

"You're wise and kind," said Sarah, "but I'm not a teenager with stars in my eyes. I only know that I can't face the noise of sewing machines, and a dreary bedsitter, not after my dashing life from one photographic session to another, and the TV work in commercials. I wore stunning clothes and I had lots of lively friends – right now those friends would give me their sympathy, but after a while they'd drift away because I no longer belong to their world, and that would be far harder for me to take than if I give it up now and I go in search of a new life. Won't you wish me luck?"

The nurse gazed at the slim figure curled on the white bed, the lamplight making a red satin cape of the lovely hair – the kind that the hairdressers tried to give to their customers by way of the henna bottle.

"What are you thinking?" Sarah's smile was whimsical.

"That maybe you're a bit like your name," her nurse replied.

"A poor little innocent, eh?"

"You may smile, Miss Innocence, but it could be true."

"I've been a model, not a member of a closed order!"

"That doesn't alter the fact, does it, that you're still only a bit of a girl. You – well, you haven't played around, have you?" The nurse bit her lip. "I mean, we know these things, when we've had someone so helpless in our hands."

"You mean I'm still a virgin?"

"Yes –"

"Is it so surprising?"

"Well, the life of a model must be rather fast, and someone with your looks must have been popular with men."

"Funnily enough a lot of men found me unapproachable, except through the eye of the camera. That probing eye found something in me that transmitted itself rather well to the magazine page and the television screen. Looks aren't everything. Perhaps I've a basically cold heart, for I feel nothing – absolutely nothing but a cold rage at the way my so-called adorer walked out on me after I told him the doctor's verdict on my foot. Lame! Lame! It was there in his eyes – as if I'd suddenly been declared a leper!"

Sarah took a contemptuous look at her bare left hand. "To think I wore his ring and said I'd be his wife! It must have been his country mansion I was in love with. It couldn't have been him! Love is supposed to be immortal, isn't it?"

"For the right man, Miss Innocence."

"Really?" Sarah's lips moved in a smile but her eyes remained like frozen green gems. "I didn't realise that nurses were romantic. I should think you see too much of the seamy side of human nature to remain in any way idealistic. Screams, moans, and bedpans must have an effect on your sensibilities?"

"Now you're being cynical," the nurse chided her. "Anyway, it will soon be time for your evening meal and I'm going to leave you to have a nice wash. Wear that pale pink bed-jacket of yours. It goes beautifully with your hair."

"And sit in solitary splendour to eat my four-course supper in this posh clinic which I can barely afford? Oh well, I suppose that's about all I can do, and with the barest luck some acquaintance will remember my existence and call in to chat for half an hour."

"It's your own fault that people stopped coming to see you. You know you snapped at them over the phone and put them off."

"And faint hearts that they are, especially when it comes

15

to sickrooms, they stayed away. Don't you see, nurse? I shrank from their sympathy, and the way they couldn't take it because I can't dance to their wild music any more. In their eyes I'm literally an invalid – a cripple – and if I see it in their eyes I shall begin to believe it myself!"

"Then it's better to be solitary," the nurse said reasonably. "You have a nice leisurely supper, and then read your Agatha Christie thriller. You know how you enjoy her books."

"That's because I'm in love with her detective. Hercule – isn't it a fluent foreign name. I wonder if my unknown employer-to-be has a such a sonorous name?"

"Miss Innocence, really!"

"Now don't go into shock, nurse. Run away to your less bothersome patients and forget you ever knew me."

"As if I could forget you, miss!" The nurse smiled in a perplexedly fond way at the girl whom the clinic staff had dubbed the girl with the apple-green eyes. Lovely, hurt, and terribly alone. No relatives to call on her, a broken career to contend with, and heaven alone knew what kind of a future lay ahead of her. She was too attractive, perhaps. Men thought they could have this living doll, and then found her impossible to even touch. The one man she had taken to had rejected her because his horse had lamed her – some men could be abominably cruel and it was to be hoped that Sarah Innocence didn't fall again into the wrong pair of masculine hands.

A hope faintly despaired of by her nurse, who gave a sigh as she left Sarah's sickroom – the room from which she would depart in a few days' time, to face life on the outside of these safe, clinical walls.

Sarah prepared for one more evening alone, washing her white skin, brushing her red hair, putting a little paint on her lips that were still a trifle pale. She stared into the mirror into her slanting green eyes and when she caught a hint of fear in them she backed away from the mirror, feeling the halting way that she walked. She who had possessed one of the most celebrated saunters of them all.

It wasn't fair. No, the silence cried back at her – it was fate.

And the fateful memory of it all rushed over her – a Friday evening call from Peter. "Look, old girl, I'm having a few pals down for the weekend and I want them to get to know you. They like to ride across the Downs first thing of a morning, to work up an appetite, so bring your breeches and a couple of cashmeres. Thank heaven you have the figure for both!"

Her figure – her seat on a horse – those were the assets most important to Peter Jameson. He had even overlooked her East End background in favour of her looks, but now she was lame and he didn't want to know.

Sarah pressed her fingers into the bones of her face. If she had been plain and bulky she wouldn't have gone in for modelling and would have been resigned to the factory life chosen for her by old Gran. But she had tasted the sweet life, and now it came hard swallowing the bitter pill of disillusion. A living doll had to be perfect in all its parts, and when it became damaged it was tossed to one side – as she had been. But the aching anger within her didn't belong to a doll it belonged to a woman, and she had to limp out of this place at the end of the week and face life.

The lonely life of a model who had toppled from the heights to fall with a broken foot that would never truly mend again. She had wept at first, still weak from shock and surgery, but now the tears had set like ice and Sarah had drawn on the courage that East-Enders learn to store up in their very bones and she looked ahead of her with challenging eyes.

Her supper as usual was a solitary one, enlivened by a brief visit from one of the young Sisters, and after she had left and the dinner tray had been taken away, Sarah took another long look at the intriguing advertisement in her magazine.

Finally she set it aside and took her writing-case from the bedtable and unscrewed the cap of her fountain-pen. She wrote to the box number at Bride Lane in London and stated that she was English born, single, in good health and desirous of going abroad to live. Then, with a tiny, almost caustic twist to her lip, Sarah withdrew from the flap of the writing-case a recent photograph of herself. It showed her in a champagne silk dress with a white Serbian fur slung around her shoulders. Her gleaming red hair was arranged high in a tiara style and around her slim white throat were the stunning black pearls which she had been hired to display for the duchess who was selling them. The Black Prince pearls, said to have been brought back from the Crusades long ago by one of King Richard's knights, and rumoured to have been snatched from the throat of a Saracen lady.

Sarah gazed at the photograph as if looking at a picture of a stranger. Yes, she thought. The glamour of it might appeal to these people who had placed the advertisement in order to find a lady companion. That golden girl who faced the camera so confidently, so gracefully, who had come to answering such an appeal like some shy spinster who feared that life was passing her by.

The situation was both piquant and unreal. As she sealed the envelope and addressed it, she half-hoped that she would hear nothing at all from the people to whom she wrote. With an assumption of carelessness she placed the stamped addressed envelope on her bedtable, and then settled down for the night. She slept restlessly for a while, then awoke in the dense silence to lie sleepless for about an hour, going over in her mind all that had happened in the past six weeks. She lived again that toss from the saddle of Grey Lady, cringed in her bed from the memory of the pain, and felt once more the hurt and the anger when Peter Jameson told her that he was going away on a safari and felt it best that they parted as chums rather than future husband and wife.

"Keep the ring, old girl," he had said, carelessly. "It's worth a bit and will help pay your clinic bills."

"You keep the blasted thing," she had retorted, the angry Cockney back in her voice. "I'll manage to pay my own bills, thanks very much. By the way, how's Grey Lady? None the worse, I hope, for her bad temper?"

"That lady has the temper of a thoroughbred," he had rejoined nastily. "Your trouble, old girl, is that you weren't born in the saddle."

"No, I was born in a damned bed," she had shouted at him. "And now get out of my expensive sickroom and out of my sight, and take your phoney ring with you!"

"Phoney!" he had snorted. "Look who's talking, a common little snip from the Roman Road posing as a girl of class. As a matter of fact my family weren't too pleased about our engagement, and we could have avoided this scene if you'd taken your medicine like a lady."

"You take it!" And so saying Sarah had grabbed the glass of water and peppermint from her bedtable and slung the liquid full in his high-nosed face. He had stormed out, wet and furious, and after her initial sense of triumph Sarah had broken down and wept like a child. It wasn't because her heart was broken, but because she visualised loneliness ahead of her, and nothing can be more bleak than that. The ring had lain there on the floor where she'd flung it, the pearl like a teardrop, the jade like her wet, tear-darkened eyes.

When the nurse came and found her crying, Sarah sobbed angrily that she wanted the ring placed in a box and sent to her ex-fiancé's flat at Palace Yard Mews.

"Do it – now!" she had begged. "Get it out of my sight!"

Sarah stared into the darkness and was pleased she had

19

had the backbone to return the expensive and meaningless ring. If she had kept it and sold it, then a substantial part of her bills would have been paid with the money that it fetched. She would have been financially better off, but minus her pride.

Sarah couldn't deny that her pride meant a lot to her. It had enabled her to be scornful of the affairs that certain other models indulged in . . . that, she knew, was why Peter had proposed to her, because she wouldn't lower those standards which old Gran had drilled into her. "Starve, my girl," the old lady had once said, "rather than become soiled goods on the counter. Become that and no decent man will ever look at you, or respect you. Respect can keep you warm on a cold day, and keep you cool towards men who only want to play around with your affections."

It now seemed to Sarah that desire made liars of men. It made them say all sorts of things they didn't really mean. "I'd give an arm to cherish you!" That was what Peter had said, and like a little fool with her head in the clouds she had believed him.

Cherish was such a beautiful word, but he had cheapened it for her and if any man ever used it to her again she would slap the word from his lips . . . what had Shakespeare written? *Like fire and powder, which as they kiss consume.* It sounded exciting, explosive, but it never really happened. Love was a cruel trap. Love wasn't the opal gem of life, a mixture of lights and shades, of dazzling colours, passionate, pure and everlasting.

Love was an illusion, and it was a good thing she had found it out and couldn't be hurt or fooled by it ever again.

She finally drifted off into a sound sleep that lasted the remainder of the night. She awoke to a cup of tea, and the absence from her bedtable of the letter she had written to Bride Lane.

The sinews of her heart seemed to go tight, she felt sure

that in the sober daylight she would have destroyed the letter and put out of her mind the crazy notion of applying for the job of companion in what was probably a foreign household. But someone had carried it off to post, and she must face the realisation that she might receive a reply in the next day or so, perhaps from a man who might be some sort of a sadistic monster who wanted to get a woman at his mercy. How better than to advertise for someone who might be foolish enough to go to him, thinking he had a wife or daughter who wanted companionship.

Sarah drank her tea and tried to forget about the letter, and she partially succeeded in the few days that followed, during which she saw again the surgeon who had operated on her, a rather handsome man who held her hand and assured her that it wouldn't affect her life as a woman to have a slight limp. Sarah could have said that it drastically affected her career as a model, but he would brush that aside, this man who dealt in life and death and regarded her as one of his successes.

"You've been a very brave girl," he told her. "Don't lose your grit out there in the great big world."

"I'll try not to," she said bravely. "Thank you for all you've done for me."

"Happy to do it, especially for a decorative young person like yourself." His grey eyes skimmed her hair. "Have you made any plans for the future?"

"One or two," she said, with rather more lightness than she felt. "I shall keep away from horses in future – the bare thought of riding gives me the horrors."

"Ah, but you mustn't be afraid of what has hurt you," he said. "You must challenge it – face it, then the fear and the horror will go away. Riding is good exercise and I imagine you look good in the saddle." He permitted himself a smile as he pressed her hand and rose to his feet. "You leave the clinic in the morning, don't you?"

She nodded and felt a clutch of apprehension at her

heart. The world beyond these walls did seem a big place – a rather empty place now she was cut loose from her old life of modelling sessions, filming at the commercial studios, invitations to cocktail parties, and dancing at clubs and on the decks of Thameside yachts.

The bright life of the successful butterfly, able to flit airily from one honeyed hour to the next.

A different mode of life yawned ahead of her, and Sarah was afraid.

"Let me wish you luck," said her surgeon. "You'll take a holiday, of course? You rather need one after what you've been through."

"I – I shall try," she said, knowing that it was hopeless in her present state of financial distress to contemplate a holiday. What she had to do was to set about finding digs and moving out of her tower flat, a prospect that filled her with a sense of gloom, for it was a charming flat with its own small balcony overlooking St. James' Park.

"You must indeed try," he said. "And now I'll bid you goodbye as in the morning I shall be tied up in the operating theatre. Come and see me at my consulting rooms in about six weeks' time and I'll check on that ankle. How does it feel when you walk? Does it still ache?"

"Slightly," she said, "but not half as bad as it was. It's the – the limping part that I can't get used to. It makes me feel conspicuous."

"Nonsense," he said. "It's barely noticeable, and as I told you once before, young woman, it could have been your neck and that would have laid you flat on your back for months and afterwards you'd have spent your life in a wheelchair. You must be grateful for that limp. Far better than a bent neck, eh?"

"Oh yes." She shuddered at the graphic picture which he painted. It was true, she wasn't helpless, but she was out of work, and she just couldn't face the factory life she had left six years ago. A dive off Thames Bridge was preferable to that!

"Then go on being a brave girl," he said. "Go to the seaside and get your lungs filled with good bracing air. Do you the world of good."

He smiled at her from the doorway, and then was gone, a man of purpose, with an assured place in the scheme of life. He couldn't know how if felt to be adrift, with no sure anchor to cling to. She had her health, and she'd been given back most of her strength, but nothing could alter the fact that a lame model was an outcast from her kind of world – a world where grace of movement was as important as wings were to the lovely tiger moth.

The day sped and her packing was all done. She had to take a pill to get her to sleep that night – a night that felt like her last secure one for a long time to come. Morning brought the clinic secretary to her room, and Sarah wrote out the cheques that left her deposit account almost depleted.

"I hope you've enjoyed your stay with us, Miss Innocence," said the secretary, as if this were a high-class hotel instead of a place where the sick and the lame came hopefully to be mended. "I expect you're pleased to be going home, aren't you?"

"Oh yes," said Sarah, and she tilted her chin and tried not to let it show that she was shaking in her shoes. No longer the high-heeled ones of the old days, but sensible pigskin with little brass buckles. One of the nurses had gone out and bought them for her, and they seemed very much a symbol to Sarah of Cinderella's lost slipper.

The goodbyes were said, and the small gifts of money were pressed into the hands which had nursed her so well. Sarah stepped into the taxi that waited for her, and her eyes were blurred by tears. It felt awful to be letting go of kindness, a wrench which she felt as the cab sped away from the swing doors of the clinic and headed along Baker Street.

There would be no one at the flat to welcome her, and

23

her key grating in the lock had a lonely sound. She stepped inside to the faint lingering aroma of the perfume she always used and would no longer be able to afford – and there on the green doormat was a slim white envelope, with her name and address in neat type on the face of it.

She put down her suitcase and stooped to pick up the letter – the postmark was E.C.4., and she knew at once that it came from Bride Lane in reply to her crazy request to that unknown gentleman living in a foreign climate.

Sarah wildly told herself that she wouldn't open it, but of their own volition her fingers seemed to tear at the sealed flap, and she stood there in the small foyer of her flat scanning the few lines of neat typing on the notepaper headed by the name and crest of a certain famous hotel in Piccadilly.

The letter requested that she go to the hotel at ten in the morning precisely, to be interviewed by a gentleman who went by the name of Sidi Kezam Zabayr. The day of her interview was Tuesday next, and it would be appreciated if she were punctual.

As if – just as if she were going to be offered the job!

CHAPTER TWO

It was all very circumspect. They met in the palm-treed lounge of the Fitzroy, and this distinguished Arab in the impeccable grey suit ordered coffee and cakes for two.

Then he sat down in the woven cane sofa facing Sarah's chair and for about a minute he silently studied her with eyes that were very dark and shrewd. "Yes, you very much resemble your photograph," he said at last. "You are of good family, *hein*? You have excellent facial bones, and I can see from your hands that you do not work for a living."

"But I – " The words died on Sarah's lips – well, why not? If he wanted to think her a social butterfly, what harm did it do to act the part? This was only a game, after all. She had no real intention of getting so involved in this scheme that she wouldn't be able to make a retreat when the moment came to discreetly do so. She had come here out of sheer curiosity – that's what Sarah told herself as the waiter brought coffee to the table and it was poured into the square white cups.

"You will have a cake?" enquired her host. "Or are you like most European women, on a diet to keep your svelte figure?"

"No, I've never needed to diet," she said truthfully. "I burn up energy and keep slim quite naturally. I'm one of the lucky m –"

There she broke off again and sliced her fork into a peach pastry. It was awful, but she kept forgetting that she was no longer a celebrated model. She was a has-been – a lame duck, and as soon as the shrewd eyes of Sidi Kezam Zabayr noticed this, he would give her one of those polite oriental bows and leave her to limp out of the Fitzroy into the teeming traffic of London, there to wait for a bus because she could no longer afford the fare of a taxi cab.

"The women of my country are very fond of sweet things," he murmured, leaning back in the sofa and watching her over the rim of his coffee cup. "In fact it was a practice of the *seraglio* to fatten the new additions on plenty of cream and *cous-cous*. Tell me, Miss Innocence, have you ever been to Maroc?"

"Morocco?" she exclaimed. "Why, no! It's a very colourful place, isn't it?"

"It is a very large place, and some parts of it are still as feudal as in the old days of the Barbary pirates." He said this almost deliberately, as if testing her in some subtle way. "You are a very modern young woman, if a man may be permitted to judge from the way that you dress and wear your hair. The hair, it is a natural colour, *hein*? Not applied from a bottle of henna?"

"No, indeed!" Sarah looked a little indignant. "My hair is far from being artificial."

"Excellent," he said, and deep in his eyes a glint of amusement seemed to stir, as if it amused him that he had sparked off a little of her redhead's temper. "And may I hope that there is nothing else about you that is artificial? One can never tell in this day and age if a woman's body is her own or the result of expert padding in certain areas of her anatomy. From where I sit you appear to have a natural shape, though a little on the slender side, if I may say so?"

"You may indeed say so," she rejoined. "I'd hate to be stout."

"Ah yes, from the flash of the green eyes you would undoubtedly hate to be an ounce over weight. To Europeans this slenderness is a sign of beauty, eh?"

"European men do seem to prefer slimness to obesity in women," she agreed.

"The fact of the matter is, Miss Innocence, that the man

for whom I act as agent in this matter of the companion is not a European. You gathered that much for yourself, *hein*?"

"I – I wasn't sure," she said, and her eyes ran wildly over the swarthy face of her host. "He's a Morroccan, then?"

"He is a Berber, like myself." A sudden stern note came into the deep, throaty voice, and suddenly this man was very foreign despite his excellent command of English and his perfectly cut European suit. The moustache across his upper lip seemed to tauten, and a frown was cleft between his black eyebrows. "We of pure Berber blood count ourselves as a tribe apart from the multi-mixtured races of Casablanca and Fez and some other regions of Maroc. We have our own culture and our own history, and living as we do in the desert itself we remain less tainted by the so-called civilization of city life. You comprehend?"

"Berber," she said. "Isn't it a synonym for barbarian?"

The dense eyes glittered and Sarah suddenly felt there was danger in the air of this lounge in the heart of London. It seemed to waft in from miles away, from a place where the palm trees towered into the hot skies, and the scent of the *seraglio* mingled with the aroma of hot dark coffee.

"True," he murmured. "Very true, Miss Innocence. So you have read about the desert even if you have never been there?"

"I imagine most women have read about the desert," she replied. "One way or another, in sultry novels or in articles by journalists who have travelled there. I think I read about it in a book by Burton the explorer. He lived like an Arab for a time, didn't he?"

"Quite so, and so did another famous Englishman. You know of El Laurans of Arabia, eh? The great soldier with the Saracen blue eyes who slew his enemies as the Arabs slew them, straight across the throat and without mercy."

27

Sarah gave a shiver and knew that she had walked in here to play a game, but it wasn't a game at all. She wanted to snatch up her handbag and dash from the Fitzroy into the noisy daylight, where people hurried by with mundane matters on most of their minds. Out there lay sanity, but in here the atmosphere had quickened with figures from another time, another place – Burton of the burning eyes, and Lawrence in his white robes with fanatical blue eyes sweeping the desert ranges he had conquered with an army of brigands riding fast horses and camels across the limitless spaces that smoked in the sun. The legendary Arabs, who sleep upon the sands and follow the stars.

Her fingers clenched her bag and she half-rose from her chair.

"Are you going to run away," the *sidi* half-mocked her. "A woman with red hair should have more spirit than that, scared away by those English ghosts who were unafraid of the desert – and what it held."

"What does it hold – for me?" she asked.

"I am not a sand *sorcière*. I can only tell you that you are considered for the position in the household of the Khalifa of Beni Zain, but whether you are chosen remains for him to say."

Sarah stared into the dark eyes of Kezàm Zabayr, and she could feel the startled beating of her heart. "If – if this man is so lordly, why does he need to advertise for anyone?" she demanded.

"Why, Miss Innocence, do you reply to such an advertisement? You with your obvious attractions?"

"I – I did it for a lark," she said defiantly.

"A – lark?"

"A joke. I'm not serious about any of it – as if I could be!"

"I think you delude yourself when you say that. I believe you are intrigued by the idea, and possibly the kind of woman who likes to spend money but now finds

herself somewhat insolvent." The dark eyes were incredibly shrewd and knowing, and it flashed through Sarah's
mind that he was like the Grand Vizier at some fantastic
court of Barbary, hidden away in the mountains where life
still went on as it had done in the past. She could tell that
he was reading her thoughts in her eyes, and she glanced
away from him, giving him the haughty line of her young,
flawless profile. Even so she could feel him staring at her,
studying her as a botanist might a butterfly on a pin.

"Come, Miss Innocence," he murmured, "don't pretend
that it didn't catch you like a magnet, the idea of serving
a man of means. And why not? You have beauty to sell,
so why not sell it?"

"In your Barbary slave market?" she gasped.

"If you wish to call it that," he agreed. "Let us say that
your kind of woman – attractive, fairly intelligent, chic,
highly sensitive, would be unlikely to be found in our part
of the world. The tourists come to Fez and Casablanca,
but they aren't up to – standard, shall I say? For the most
part they have husbands trailing behind their loud,
demanding voices, and they have hardly the requirements
to suit my lord Zain Hassan, high lord of Beni Zain,
grand master of a tribe that inhabits a rambling section of
the Barbary desert, in whose veins the blood of pirates
chases that of Saracen lions. It was his whim, for he has a
certain ironical turn of humour, to place the advertisement
in one of your high-class magazines. "We shall," he said,
"either get ourselves a horse-faced spinster, or a blonde
adventuress."

Sarah gave the Khalifa's agent a bitter-sweet smile.
"And instead you got a red-haired adventuress," she said.
"I'll admit that I'm broke. I'm down to my last few pounds
and I'd like to get away from England, but not this way,
thank you. Not in the household of some old caliph of a
desert tribe."

"Old?" Kezam Zabayr raised a black scimitar of an

29

eyebrow. "The Khalifa Zain Hassan is a man in the prime of life, with many demands on his time and attention. That he has chosen this unorthodox method of selecting an employee for a not inconsiderable position in his household is due entirely to his admiration for British methods of female education – he regards women of your country as above average intelligence. He gave me the task of selecting a British girl to be presented to him, and now I have met you I wish to present you. It is as simple as that, *mademoiselle*."

"Simple?" She looked at him in astonishment. "The whole thing has taken on complications I didn't dream of when I applied for the job."

"Complications? I don't think I understand you." His eyebrow went a little higher. "The woman who is chosen for the position will be very much honoured, and the tribe will respect the Khalifa's decision in this matter of what is important to him in his own tent, as we say."

"He lives in a *tent*?" she exclaimed, and in an instant she visualised one of those long black nomadic structures on the desert sands, filled with smoke from the cooking fires, with a number of children playing among the rolled up carpet bedding.

"When in the desert, but his residence at Beni Zain is a *kasbah*," she was informed. "In England you would call it a castle, *hein*? The stronghold of a lord."

Sarah reached for her cup of coffee and felt as if she had wandered into the realms of the Arabian Nights. So this gentleman of means was a feudal Berber, and she couldn't help but harbour the suspicion that he fancied a girl of white skin in his *serayi*. Being in his prime could mean that he was anything between fifty and seventy; it was well known that men of the East retained a lively interest in the female of the species.

"I seem to have taken your breath away." Kezam Zabayr smiled briefly.

30

"That is putting it mildly, *monsieur*." Sarah didn't quite know what else to call him, and her left foot had begun to ache, reminding her that what this man offered was a kind of security, fantastic and a little unnerving, but somehow not so awful as being on social benefit in a back street bedroom. Oh dear, was this how Eve had felt when the golden-voiced serpent held out the apple so temptingly?

"Is the idea of working in Maroc so outlandish, Miss Innocence? Is that what you mean when you refer to complications, that you now find that your place of employment would be in the desert, and your master would be a Berber? Has this lark, as you call it, now taken on a more sinister aspect in your eyes?"

"You – you don't believe in sparing a girl's blushes, do you?" Sarah sorted about in her handbag, in need of one of those tiny tablets that relieved the pain in her foot. The *sidi* misunderstood and proffered a gold cigarette case.

"No, thanks, I don't smoke." She snapped shut her bag, remembering in time that she mustn't take a pain-killer in front of this man – not if she really harboured hopes of landing this fantastic job. If she popped in a pill he would take her for a drug addict, or someone who was sick. The sickness was over, but the occasional gnawing ache still bothered her.

"You are nervous." He gave a tolerant shrug of his shoulders and lit a gold-tipped cigarette for himself. He exhaled smoke in a deliberate way, blowing it away from her with discreet good manners. "It is understandable, and yet the letter sent to you stated my name and you could see that you would be dealing with a man of the East. Come, it was no lark that brought you here, *mademoiselle*. You came because you prefer cheesecake to bread and cheese. I am right, *hein*?"

"I'm naturally concerned to find a well-paid job," she admitted. "I – would I be companion to the Khalifa's wife – or wives?"

31

The dark brows contracted; he seemed amused. "The Khalifa is a widower, but he has sisters and he has decided that he wishes them to have the benefit of knowing a woman – shall we say of the world?"

"His sisters?" Sarah looked surprised. "Are they enclosed in a harem, and would I be expected to share that kind of a life?"

"They dwell in the *serayi,* the female section of the *kasbah,* but they have the freedom of all that part of the house and you may take it from me that it is a large one. It might take a week or more for a woman to explore all of it."

"I see." Despite her misgivings Sarah began to feel intrigued. "They don't go veiled or anything like that, do they? You know, little bits of Eastern delight, kept in seclusion and expected to be sweet and submissive. I – I could be a disrupting influence, couldn't I?"

"There is a chance of that." Kezam Zabayr flicked his dark eyes over her hair, worn smoothly at her neck but still not entirely subdued. "I wonder if I would be wise to present you to my lord Zain Hassan?"

"Why, is he a tyrant who can't endure a little fire and spirit in the opposite sex?"

This time the dark eyes narrowed and lost their faint glimmer of amusement. She saw the generous lips go a little thin beneath the line of the moustache. "That is the trouble with European women, they have sharp tongues and malicious minds. You may not be suitable after all, Miss Inocence, and I think we will conclude our discussion."

"Now who's being faint-hearted?" she murmured. "If Zain Hassan is such a man among men, then he shouldn't mind if a mere woman stands up to him. It was his idea, after all, to hire a European companion for his sisters. If he wants them to remain subdued, then he shouldn't let a woman of the world into their domain. It would surely be like letting a cat into a mousehole."

"Your eyes are green as a cat's," he mused. "Could you accept a man's complete authority over you, Miss Innocence? It is the ruling of the Koran that a woman be humble, modest, obedient and tender."

"And what of men?" she asked. "Are they given the freedom to be arrogant, masterful, high-handed and even a little cruel?"

"If a man is not a tiger, then who respects him?"

"If a man is a tiger, who dares to approach him?"

"A clever woman can make a tiger purr."

"All of which, *monsieur*, means that Zain Hassan won't be led by the whiskers, I take it?"

"*Non*." The word was curt, explicit, and somehow it conjured up an image of a man who strode arrogantly through the courts of his castle, his robes flying around him, a flare to the nostrils of his hawkish nose . . . a master whom no one dared to defy, even in this matter of finding a suitable woman to give his sisters companionship and bring into their secluded lives something of the outside world.

"Is he fearfully rich?" Sarah asked casually.

"Rich enough, *mademoiselle*." The dark eyes swept from her hair to her slim hands, one of which was drumming slim fingers on the edge of the cane table. "You like good things, eh, but in a discreet fashion? Your suit is hand-sewn, your perfume is subtle, your hands are well-kept, and your ear-jewels are genuine and they match your eyes."

His gaze dwelt on those little drops of jade, which she had bought for herself out of her last modelling cheque.

"It is a pity you have an indiscreet mode of speech," he added.

"Am I being politely turned down for the – post?"

He frowned as he regarded her, obviously a man who preferred his women to be seen but not too often heard. "You came here, did you not, merely out of curiosity, with no serious intention of being a companion?"

"I had no idea it was an Eastern potentate who required one," she said. "Perhaps I thought that the advertiser might be a planter – they still do exist in tropical climates, or have I been reading too many novels?"

"May I say, Miss Innocence, that you don't strike me as an intellectual woman, or one who needs to find her escape between the covers of a book. I am curious to know why you even thought of applying for the position."

"I – I'm bored," she said, but she was also nervous, and aware that she didn't really want to walk away into a bleak future. This one at least offered change and challenge. "And I am very broke – "

"Are you a virgin?" he asked her abruptly.

"Yes – " Sarah gave him a shocked look. "But what has that to do with you, may I ask?"

"This companion to the Khalifa's sisters must be a good woman. Tell me, would you take your oath on that, Miss Innocence?"

"Yes!" Her green eyes flashed, but she bit back the indiscreet words that came to her lips. "Of course."

"There is no 'of course' about it when one is dealing with the emancipated European woman," he said, a thread of scorn in his voice. "Virginity would be the jewel beyond price in a woman of your looks, and I am willing to believe you. Are you waiting for a rich man to come along?"

Sarah could feel her eyes smouldering with temper, and she truly wished that she could afford to tell this man to go to hell. It stung that he seemed to hit so close to the truth – it had been Peter Jameson's large house in the country and his connections with one of the big banking firms which had swayed her, along with those lazily elegant ways of his, and the way he spoke. Yes, it had to be true that she had been holding out for a man of means, and had kept herself aloof from casual love affairs because after a time it showed if a girl was playing around with men.

It showed in her manner, her eyes, and in the way her looks lost their freshness.

"All right," she said defiantly. "Is it such a crime for a girl to set some value by the way she looks, and to want something more from life than drudgery?"

"Drudgery?" Kezam Zabayr arched a black eyebrow. "What would you know about that, *mademoiselle*?"

"Nothing," she lied. "But when a girl runs out of money she sees it ahead of her, if she's the sort who doesn't care to sell herself to every Tom, Dick and Harry."

"But you wouldn't hesitate to work for a gentleman of means?" he drawled. "Of course you wouldn't, otherwise you and I would never have met like this to discuss whether I shall present you to the Khalifa, or dismiss you as unsuitable. That you have kept your purity is quite a temptation, Miss Innocence."

"Thank you," she said coldly. "It hasn't been calculated – I'm not a robot without feelings."

"Really? To an Arab a woman is a thing of joy, but she is without a soul."

"How charming! A sort of doll, to be put away in its cupboard when not required."

"Pampered, kept in seclusion, and greatly cared for if she should bear a son. If she does that she is assured that she will never be put away from her husband, even if his eyes should fall upon another woman. You comprehend?"

"Without a shadow of a doubt." A note of ice tinkled in Sarah's voice and it was at this moment that she wished she had the courage, and the currency, to rise and walk away from this table. But she was as mesmerised as a stoat by a snake, and she knew it.

"You must understand, Miss Innocence, that my master would have complete authority over you, which you would not be able to contest. Could you accept such authority?"

No, she wanted to retort. I'd want to fight it like mad!

"I – I suppose I'd have to," she said, with an assumption of sweetness. "I only hope the seclusion wouldn't be too confining – I suppose I'd be allowed out to see the shops and visit the *hammam*? I understand that Eastern women make quite a party of going to the steam baths?"

His lips faintly quirked. "You would not be quite a prisoner, and as you are European a few concessions would be made in order to keep you – sweet." His eyes gleamed, as if he well knew that she was making an effort to be nice to him.

"Am I now reconsidered for the presentation?" she asked.

"Perhaps. You are young and obviously you can be charming when it suits you, and you might appeal to the Khalifa's sisters."

"When would the presentation take place, and where?"

"It would take place at Beni Zain, when you would meet the Khalifa at the same time as the other women –"

"Others?" she broke in. "Just how many?"

"About half a dozen."

"Like a – a damned slave market!" Sarah looked dumb-founded. "You implied that I'd be the only applicant – "

"You led yourself to believe that, Miss Innocence." He stressed her surname, and carefully brushed ash from his trousered knee. "It's quite usual – there must be a selection of applicants for such a man, and he is far too occupied to arrange the matter for himself. You will be the only Englishwoman at the mart."

Sarah closed her eyes in a kind of stunned wonder at what she had got herself involved in – she couldn't go through with it, to stand like some chattel on display, for this Berber chief to study as if she were a filly he might select for his stable.

"No – " She shook her red head. "It isn't my kind of thing!"

"I suspected that you would lose your nerve," he said,

a trifle sarcastically. "I saw it coming, Miss Innocence, from the moment I joined you at this table. What a pity you lack the gumption to compete with these other women, for there is every chance that you might catch the Khalifa's attention. Such good bones, and eyes most unusual in an English woman. Have you no confidence in your own appeal?"

"You talk as if this were a beauty contest," she retorted. "Does a companion have to be some sort of a raving beauty? Anyway, the whole thing is – barbaric. Six women on display for one man – who the devil does he think he is?"

"The tribal chieftain of a region as large as this island, from which you wanted to get away. It would be an adventure, would it not?"

Sidi Kezam Zabayr sat back in his seat and studied her from beneath the lowered lids of his Eastern eyes.

An adventure, she thought. A lark that left her slightly shaken instead of eager. How on earth could she, a lame duck, hope to compete with those other women from all parts of the world; women who might have qualifications that a girl who left school at sixteen could never have acquired? It just wasn't worth the journey, for this Khalifa Zain Hassan would require someone a lot less tranquil than she could ever pretend to be. She couldn't hide her true nature as she might hide her flame-red hair under a dark snood; nor could she hide the fact that she limped when she walked.

"Your fare will be paid to Maroc, and from the airport you will be taken by car to the railroad to catch the Moroccan Express into the region of Beni Zain. If you aren't thought suitable, your fare home will be paid. It is worth the trip even if you lose the contest, eh?"

Something tingled in Sarah's veins when he said that, and she caught again that illusory whiff of the far desert, where it didn't seem so strange that a Berber chief should

37

send his emissaries to find women for him . . . in whatever capacity he required them.

"There's every chance," she said drily, "that the Khalifa will like several of the women – what will he do in that event?"

The *sidi* regarded the tip of his cigarette and in his eyes that shrewd little light was glinting. "Only one companion is required, and she will have to be the best of the bouquet."

"I see." Sarah met those dark, knowing, utterly foreign eyes. "What a waste, when the runners-up could be requisitioned into your master's harem." Then, looking down at the table, she dared to say: "He has a harem, no doubt?"

"My lord Zain Hassan has no harem, Miss Innocence. He is foremost a man who puts his people before his own pleasures, and secondly he is something of a warrior. He prefers the battle of wits with certain of our traditional enemies to the softening influence of the *serayi*. In many respects he is an unusual man, but there isn't a member of the Beni Zain who would dispute his leadership. It is because of his extensive interest in the tribe itself that he leaves certain matters in my hands."

"Are your hands very capable, *monsieur*?"

"I believe so, *mademoiselle*. Those in the trust of Zain Hassan do well to be competent, for he has little patience with mediocrity."

"He sounds a hard man. He's a widower, you say, but aren't Moslems allowed to have three wives?"

"Of course, but the Khalifa has not found time to marry more than one, and she is unfortunately lost to him. That is why he desires companionship for his sisters – when again a woman takes the eye of Zain Hassan it will be because he must have sons for the Beni Zain. Honour enough for any female!"

"You mean she would be wasting her time to expect

38

to be loved?" It was a daring thing to say in the circumstances, but Sarah couldn't help feeling curious about these people and their strangely different ways.

Sidi Kezam Zabayr merely looked at her, and it was answer enough.

Sarah dabbed at her lips with a table napkin and couldn't help but feel churned up inside and more and more intrigued by this barbaric Zain Hassan who would choose a woman for himself as other men might select an overcoat or a necktie. It was incredible, and when she got home she would laugh at all this and dismiss it from her mind . . . but oh, would she?

She watched as the Khalifa's emissary opened his wallet and took from it a tawny envelope. "This," he said, "holds a single ticket on the Continental Airways flight to Casablanca leaving tomorrow evening. Do you want it, Miss Innocence?"

Sarah stared at the ticket in his dark-skinned hand . . . her heart hammered and she knew that the apple was being offered and that if she took a bite from it she might fly to Eden . . . and have that holiday her surgeon had talked about!

"You're tempting me, *monsieur,*" she said. "You have found my weak spot, haven't you?"

"I usually do," he murmured. "You want more than anything else to get away from your own country at this moment in time, and this ticket in my hand represents your means of escape. I am tempted to wonder what has occurred in your life that makes it so imperative that you get away – has some man broken your heart?"

"Not my heart but my self-confidence," she replied. "Dare I hope that your lord Zain Hassan will pass me over for one of those other women he is to be offered? I'd like to see your country, but I don't think I'd make a suitable companion. My temperament isn't docile enough for that."

"Do you gamble, *mademoiselle*?"

"I have done so," she admitted.

"Have you had much luck at the tables of chance?"

"Now and again I've won a little money – but we aren't talking about money, are we?"

"In a manner of speaking, *mademoiselle*. You asked if the Khalifa was a rich man, and that must surely mean that you are looking for the security which money offers. This air ticket could be your passport to the freedom which being generously employed gives to a woman."

"I daresay you'd call me a sentimentalist, *monsieur,* if I said that it's probably being loved that makes a woman really secure. But I also believe that it's incredibly hard to find that elusive thing called love, and somehow I don't expect to find it. I suppose if I'm a cynic I should reach out and take that ticket?"

"I will meet you halfway." He extended the envelope across the table and it was steady as steel in his dark fingers. "Come, woman of the red hair, take it and prove the saying that fire in the hair means fire in the soul."

"I want to take it," she admitted, "but I can't promise what my reaction would be if your lord Zain Hassan – wanted me."

"Throw the dice, Miss Innocence, and let the fates decide if it should fall on your number or that of someone else. *Mektub*, we say in the East. It is written, or it is not. Let this ticket be your magic carpet to the gardens of Barbary."

"Are they hanging gardens?" she asked, and a wistful note crept into her faintly husky voice.

"Hanging cliffs, *mademoiselle*, where the glories of the morning hang their mauve petals."

"You speak like a poet, Sidi Kezam."

"Many desert people are poets, are you not aware of that?"

"Poet-warriors who love to fight. That's the truth,

40

isn't it, *monsieur*?"

"Don't you like to fight yourself, *mademoiselle*?" His smile just showed the edge of his teeth. "Don't be so sure that Zain Hassan requires a docile woman."

"But you said – you said that all he required was a woman who will be quietly obedient to his demands – or words to that effect."

"I said, Miss Innocence, that the Koran requires that a woman should be obedient. In truth my lord Zain Hassan is something of an enigma to even those who are close to him. Let us say that he has inherited the traits of the warrior who fathered him – a man held in great awe by those who fought alongside him. Needless to say after he was born the husband of his mother had her strangled – "

"What?" Sarah looked at the *sidi* with incredulous eyes.

"She had committed adultery, Miss Innocence, and the punishment is a very severe one."

"Don't you mean a barbarous one?" she gasped.

"It is justice in the desert." And quite deliberately he dropped the tawny envelope beside her plate. "Dare you pick it up?"

Sarah's every instinct told her that she should ignore the envelope . . . leave it where it was and make her retreat from the Fitzroy. Her mind instructed her, but her body didn't move. She sat there and the tawny envelope seemed to grow and grow until she felt that the tides of the desert had swept in and swirled around her. Even yet if she struggled she could get away and be gone in moments from this hotel lounge which had become a place of dangerous temptation.

"Take it." It was a whisper, an enticement from the very heart of the land where Eve had listened and fallen from innocence into the arms of passion.

"You'll regret this," Sarah told herself, as she picked up the envelope and felt the ticket with trembling fingers. A ticket to Casablanca, the gateway of the desert, where women had no souls and where men were the absolute masters.

"And now I have some other business to which I must attend." The *sidi* rose to his feet. "Stay a while longer, *mademoiselle*. I will instruct the waiter to bring a fresh pot of coffee. We will meet again, eh? *Mais certainement!*"

He seemed almost to smile, and then his fingers touched his brow, lips and breast and he was gone from the table and a moment more from the lounge.

Sarah was left alone . . . clutching a ticket that could take her far away from England . . . if she had the nerve to use it.

French coffee was brought to her and she sat lost in her thoughts as she stirred brown sugar into the dark depths of the brimming cup. An hour ago she had sat here waiting to hear what kind of a man had paid for that advertisement, and at no time during that hour had Kezam Zabayr been aware that he was talking to a woman who had a physical imperfection. Yes! A wicked little smile lit Sarah's green eyes, rekindling the gemlike quality that the camera always caught so well. Her lips joined that smile in her eyes and the tremor had gone from her hands as she tucked into her handbag the tawny envelope which held a ticket to faraway Morocco. Then she finished her coffee and left the Fitzroy, and as she walked out into the drizzling rain of the autumnal day she glanced up at the grey sky and felt the wetness on her face.

The skies over the desert would be incredibly blue and the sun would be gloriously warm . . . yes, she needed a holiday, and her very lameness would safeguard her from falling into the hands of this barbaric desert prince . . . high lord of a desert fiefdom where his word was law and his whip had only to stir in his hand to bring his people to heel.

As Sarah made her way to the bus stop she couldn't help wondering what Gran would have said had she known that

42

her granddaughter was thinking of going to one of those foreign countries which Gran had distrusted so much, to take part in a slave auction . . . it couldn't be called anything else, could it?

CHAPTER THREE

THE sky was burning with heat as the passengers came out
of the airport, to be greeted by friends or quickly whisked
off to one of the waiting cabs by a *dragoman,* those fast-
talking, turbaned porters who had such an instinct for
picking the dollar visitors and ignoring young women
who were obviously bewildered by the noise and the
blazing sunlight.

Sarah clutched her suitcase and her handbag and stood
there on the pavement in front of the airline building
wondering in which direction had fled all that burst of
nerve which had brought her to Casablanca.

Her suit felt crumpled and there was a run in her left
nylon – instinct had warned her that tights in this country
would only increase that sense of having landed in a
melting pot. Right now she would have given anything
for the assurance of the tall Nigerian girl who sauntered
past her to a waiting white car; she looked unutterably cool
and blasé in her lovely bright dress and golden ear-hoops,
and some of the men were staring at her as if she were a
vision.

Not a soul took any notice of Sarah, who had bunned
her hair and wore smoked glasses, and who obviously
limped as she made her way further along the hot pavement
nto the spidery shade of a tall palm tree. She might have
been invisible as she stood there and looked about her and
hoped that whoever was supposed to meet her and conduct
her to the train had not forgotten that she was arriving
today. The telegraph had promised that a car would be
at the airport to meet her, but the parking area was empty-
ing fast and soon she would be the only passenger left to
be picked up.

She felt a rush of disquiet and wondered yet again if she had been quite mad to use that ticket which Sidi Kezam Zabayr had given her, and she hoped to goodness that a car would soon arrive to waft her away from the palm tree, which barely shielded her from the sun. With every passing second she seemed to wilt a little more and felt that soon she would collapse from jet exhaustion and heat and be found in a leaf-green bundle beneath the unmoving tufted green fan of the tree. It was rather like an outsize pineapple, she thought, tufted and scaly.

How she longed right now for a glass of cool pineapple juice, and even as she gave a sigh of longing a sudden shadow fell over her and she glanced up quickly and couldn't suppress a gasp of surprise . . . or was it one of alarm?

A man stood looking at her . . . or rather he was looking her over with fierce blue eyes set beneath black brows that were made all the darker by the white *shemagh* about his head, bound with ropes. A linen tunic lay loosely corded at his brown throat, and his black breeches and leather kneeboots made her think of a tamer of tigers.

Before Sarah could control the impulse she had retreated a step or two away from him, and instantly the most mocking of looks sprang into the eyes that were so startling in that sun-clawed face. Burning blue eyes that made her flush, holding a look which told her with brutal frankness that he was not overwhelmed with admiration. His eyes raked over her, taking in her creased skirt, the run in her nylon, the unpowdered shine of her nose, and the huge rims of her smoked glasses. It was also possible that he had noticed she was lame, and Sarah had already learned the hard way how that could affect the reaction of a man, especially one who looked as fit and lithe as this tall berber.

"I assume you are Miss Innocence?" As he spoke her name his lip dented, and she noticed that he spoke English with a curious sort of menace about it, deep-throated and

45

faintly impatient. "I am to escort you to the train that will take you to Beni Zain."

"Are you the emissary of the Sidi Kezam Zabayr?" she asked, for she needed to be assured that he was a *bona fide* escort before following him anywhere. She might not be to his personal taste, but there were still stories in circulation about lone female travellers being whisked off into the desert never to be seen again, and there was something about this man that jarred her nerves and made her every instinct set up a defence against him.

"I am not a white slaver, if that is your worry," he said, with a sardonic narrowing of his eyelids that seemed to intensify the alive and searching quality of his eyes. "I know all about you, *bint,* but quite frankly you are hardly my idea of a companion for a pair of sheltered girls."

"You've got a damned nerve for a servant!" Sarah felt compelled to insult him in return, for there was something in his bearing that made the word insulting when applied to him. "If you're here to take me to the train, then do it and mind your own business."

"Temper as well, hardly another attribute of the good companion," he mocked. "I wonder if Kezam Zabayr was quite wise to recommend you to his master – one can only suppose that you were the only Englishwoman to put in an application."

"No doubt I was." Sarah flung up her chin and almost lost the large sun-glasses from off her shiny nose. She pushed them back into place with an annoyed movement of her hand – oh, for the poise that had once been hers, and the independence that would have allowed her to tell this barbarian to go and lose himself! She felt the annoyance boiling up in her and it found a prime target in this arrogant Berber – yes, he was that all right, despite the colour of his eyes. They might be crusader-blue, but their expression was utterly lawless, and his hard, almost savage bones thrust under a skin that the desert sun had

46

tanned to the toughness of a horse saddle. Dead centre in his chin was a cleft, hacked in the firm flesh and bone as if by an axe.

It was a pagan face that she looked at . . . there was no other word to describe it.

"I should imagine most Englishwomen have more sense than I have," she said self-accusingly. "I daresay I had my brains out for an airing when I boarded that jet plane last night and flew here to take part in what can only be called a slave auction."

"Ah, is that what you call it?" he drawled. "One can see that you have been letting your imagination have an airing as well. Tell me, *roumia,* if you suspected all this in London, then why didn't you stay there and be safe from the uncertain intentions of Berbers like myself? Could you not resist that certain fascination that we men of the desert have for you women of the cities?"

"You've got to be kidding," she gasped. "Do you imagine that's why I came to Morocco, on the lookout for some sheikh who'd drag me off to his tent!"

He merely looked at her, and Sarah wanted to shrink inside her jacket and cringe away from this man who said suggestive things in such perfect English, and who looked at a girl as if she had not a bit of mystery he hadn't solved long ago.

His lips parted a little in what had to be a smile; they had a bold outline and Sarah caught the almost bluish glint of his teeth. His look, then, was fierce, with a skin-thin veneer of civilized behaviour. Sarah couldn't sustain the look in his eyes and she dropped her gaze to his throat, the tawny colour seen in the pelt of a tiger.

"Yes, you were very foolish to come here, *roumia.* I have seen some of the other women and they are years older than you in experience – you, I think, must be asking for a dose of semi-rape, if not the real thing!"

His remark checked the beat of Sarah's heart for a

shocking second – had she really heard him, or was she imagining what he had just said to her?

"Don't faint!" His hand reached to her elbow and at the touch of his sunburned hand she almost cried out in protest. "You aren't used to our sunlight, so come with me before you wilt on the pavement like some shrinking violet."

Her elbow was gripped, her suitcase was taken, and it couldn't be concealed that she limped as he led her from the pavement, across the road, to where a larger black limousine waited in the shade of an awning. He thrust open the door and Sarah felt as if she were being abducted as he thrust her inside, so that she stumbled and fell on to the veloured back seat. Her suitcase was put beside her, and then the door slammed and this haughty, insolent, overbearing Berber entered through the driver's door and set the powerful engine in motion.

Sarah's breath returned as the limousine started to move. "Let me out! I'm not going with you!" she cried, and reached for the door handle.

"If you fall out you will damage yourself and I should have to deliver bruised goods to the Khalifa." He rapped the words over his shoulder even as he swung the big car around and headed it along the boulevard, where great tall palm trees stood as motionless as disciplined sentinels.

"I've changed my mind," Sarah flung at him. "I don't want to be taken to the train – I want to go home!"

"It's a trifle late in the day for a change of mind," he retorted. "Besides, I have my orders, and you wouldn't want to see me reprimanded by my angry master, would you?"

"I'd love to see it," she choked. "Turn this car around and take me back to the airport – "

"Do save your breath," he drawled. "There is nothing more unattractive than a panting, perspiring, thoroughly undignified female. Do powder your nose and relax."

48

"Blast your arrogance!" Sarah glared at the back of his cloth-covered, rope-bound head. "I didn't come here to meet with your approval, which doubtless runs to plump belly dancers with their eyes made up to resemble the gazelle. I – I'm not boarding that train. I'm not going through with this!"

"I was warned that you might prove a little – difficult," he said, and as he spoke he swung the car past tall white buildings like huge cubes of sugar in the sunlight. "That is the problem with women from the emancipated countries, they don't really know whether they want to boss, or be bossed. If they come up against an easy-going man, they end up frustrated. If they meet with one who is dominant, they immediately start to fight him. At least the belly dancer is quite happy to please her audience, and she really has a lot more dignity than the European female imitating the African ape in a gaudy nightclub."

"Thank you!" Sarah had never felt such an alarming gust of fury, so that she could have slapped this man hard round the face for his insulting remarks and not cared much if he struck her in return. He looked capable of it, and she deserved a hiding for coming here in the first place. Old Gran would have been furious with her and said she deserved a good spanking.

She gripped her handbag and could feel herself shaking with a combination of nerves and temper. Once they reached the train she would grab a taxi and return to the airport – and then her heart sank. The return fare to England would cost a lot more than she had in her wallet right now. Sheer bravado had carried her this far, but now she felt deflated and she sank back against the veloured seat in a sort of despair. It was all very well to get annoyed because a Berber struck at her British pride – but who could really blame him? If he took her for a gold-digging adventuress, then she had no one to blame but herself. All the same, for someone in the employ of the Khalifa he

49

was taking a bit of a risk with his remarks – *a risk?* Sarah's lips twisted into a wry smile. He knew as well as she that the all powerful Zain Hassan bin Hamid would flick her aside as if she were a mere crumb on the feast table. She had been brought here merely to fill the requirements of the search – that all shades of feminine skin be represented, and hers was undoubtedly very English.

She took out her powder compact and grimaced at her shiny nose. She took off the disfiguring sunglasses and ran the tiny powder puff over her cheekbones and her nose, and was unaware that the limousine had halted at some traffic signals until the driver suddenly spoke.

"You will find our climate rather hard to take for a while," he said.

Sarah shot him a startled look, and for the first time he was looking directly into her green eyes with their frame of auburn lashes. "I – I don't plan to be here all that long," she rejoined. "I'm sure we're both aware that I shan't be in the finals of this auction. Let's say I came for the ride."

"Here in the East it isn't always wise to read the book before it is opened." His eyes narrowed and as his lashes darkened those brilliant irises Sarah was confronted by a man totally of the desert. "You saw this as a way to acquire a cheap holiday, eh? You never planned to be a companion – or did your plans change when you learned that your prospective employer would be a Berber?"

"You ask too many questions for a mere *chauffeur*." She bore down scornfully on the word. "I don't have to submit to your inquisition, and I don't intend to. The lights have changed, so you'd better drive on."

"To the railway station?" he mocked. "Has it suddenly occurred to you that you are too broke to pay your way home? Oh yes, I know all about your finances, Miss Innocence. You have to auction yourself whether you like it or not."

It was true, heaven help her! She had no other alternative

50

but to go through with what she had started when she'd accepted that flight ticket and used it to come here. Otherwise she was stranded in a strange country . . . surrounded by hard, unsympathetic men like the one who drove this car, suddenly bringing it to a halt in front of a bustling and very large railway station.

He climbed out from behind the wheel and opened the door beside Sarah. "Come," he said brusquely. "Our train leaves in just a few minutes."

As she sat there staring at him, he reached in and caught her by the arm. She winced and went, if possible, even whiter in the face so that her eyes were as intensely green as emeralds. His hard fingers had closed on the vulnerable part of her arm where only yesterday at her doctor's she had been given a couple of injections for the journey to Morocco; shots against the various infections to be picked up in a foreign country with a hot climate.

"You're hurting me!" she gasped, more deeply resentful of this man than she had been even towards Peter Jameson. He had a kind of hard arrogance, even a coldness of heart, that made Sarah feel bleak. "I was a model," she wanted to fling at him. "I had dozens of friends, and I don't like being treated like a *tart*!"

"I see." He drew his hand away from her. "That is where you have received your shots, eh? My apologies if I caused you pain."

"I'm quite sure you enjoyed hurting me," she rejoined. "What do you mean about 'our' train? Don't tell me I have to travel to Beni Zain with you?"

"You do, and if you don't move yourself, *bint*, you will travel to Beni Zain by camel. Do you really suppose that you would be allowed to travel on your own? This isn't the English countryside, you know."

Evocative words that made the tears of self-pity shimmer in Sarah's eyes – what a stupid little fool she had been, flying off into the unknown and landing herself in the

51

uncaring hands of a Berber in whose eyes burned the most lawless flame she had ever seen. He could be capable of anything, for he seemed to have a stone where his heart ought to be.

"Out of the car this instant or I shall be compelled to carry you," he said, and Sarah had no option but to obey him, feeling a nervous throb in her ankle as she mounted a flight of stone steps at his side and saw waiting the Moroccan Express, a guard on the platform with the whistle almost at his lips.

"Do move yourself," her escort said curtly, and when she stumbled he abruptly swept an arm about her waist and carried her up the steps that led into the corridor of the train. They made it just in time and Sarah felt like a bundle of old clothes as she was dumped inside a first-class compartment and saw the door slide into place behind her impatient and intolerant escort.

"All the way with you?" Her lips had a sulky set to them. "It will be an enjoyable journey!"

"I am glad you think so. Be grateful that you are travelling first-class and not in the crowded section of the train where it is hot and uncomfortable." He swept a hand towards the padded seat. "Be seated, Miss Innocence, and take advantage of all that your host is paying for."

"Is he paying for his servant to travel in luxury?" she demanded. "I bet you're taking as much advantage of him as I am."

"Why not?" He shrugged his wide shoulders as he sat down on the seat opposite the one Sarah had taken. "If a man is fool enough to think he can find satisfactory an ex-model as a companion, then he deserves all that he gets. He must have his brains out for an airing, eh?"

"You're most disrespectful about him," she said, leaning back in a seat that was very comfortable, and feeling around her ankles the coolness of air-conditioning. In a way she couldn't blame this arrogant devil for riding in comfort, but she did wish she could take him down a peg or two. "Supposing I report all you've said to the Sidi Kezam Zabayr – he's obviously well in with the Khalifa and I reckon I could get you into trouble."

He laughed at that, not loudly but in a softly menacing way, somewhere in his brown throat, and leaned his robed head against the padded seat.

"Are you a little sneak as well as a little fool?" he asked. "The word of a woman out here is no more than the rustling of sand in the desert wind."

"It must be delightful to live in a country where women only feel secure if they bear sons to the almighty male." Sarah gave him a look of cool scorn, but inwardly she was not so composed. She had known even before she came here that men were the masters in the East, and this man had already intimated that she was in danger of semi-rape – or worse.

"Zain Hassan bin Hamid is a despot, isn't he?" she added. "Are you trying to pretend that he doesn't control you? In front of me you act the bully, but I bet you're as subservient as the rest of his staff when you're actually in his presence."

"Do many of your bets pay off?" he asked mockingly. "Do you really imagine that I grovel to anyone?"

"You're his paid flunkey, aren't you?" Her nose took a scornful tilt. "You take his orders and do his bidding, such as meeting me. With me you might be arrogant and domineering, because in your eyes I'm only a woman, but if the Khalifa is as all-powerful as Kezam Zabayr implied, then you do your share of grovelling. A grand master is a sort of god in the eyes of his people, isn't he? In my eyes you're only an employee of his."

Suddenly her unreasoning dislike of this aggressive and abrasive Arab seemed to grab Sarah by the throat.

"I wonder what you'd do if I were the lucky applicant for this post right inside the private quarters of the

Khalifa? I expect even he is human enough to bend his ear to a woman's whispers, and he might not like it if he thought that one of his flunkeys was being a bit too high and mighty."

Never in her life had Sarah threatened anyone, not even as a model when she had come up against the competitiveness and occasionally the spite of girls who had not been quite so successful as herself. Even with Peter Jameson she had not felt this flash of sheer temper; with him it had been bleak disappointment that a man could turn out to be so shallow underneath the show of charm. At no time with him had there been this sheer awareness of the sex warfare between men and women, but this Arab aroused it to an alarming degree.

His eyes were like twin flames under the white *shemagh*, holding hers as the train thundered beneath a tunnel.

"I do believe you would like to put a knife into me, figuratively speaking." And as the train plunged from shadow into the brilliant sunlight once more, Sarah saw the twist of a smile on his lips. "There are aspects to you, after all, that the Khalifa may find much to his liking. Despot he might be, but he doesn't care a great deal for those who make doormats of themselves."

"Really?" Despite the animosity which she felt Sarah couldn't help staring at this man's mouth, which was incredibly well shaped and in its way as lawless as those blue eyes – doubtless a heritage from the distant past, when the Crusaders had come to the desert and left behind them many a memento of a sly visit to a Saracen's harem.

"I thought," she said, "that the men of your country preferred women to be on their knees most of the time, modestly submissive and only too willing to be part of the floor coverings."

"You really mustn't believe all that you read in the novels of repressed women writers," he said sardonically.

"If desert sheiks spent all their time on the divan with a frantic woman, then their various regions would be in a state of chaos and economical collapse – as would the sheik himself."

He smiled at the image, his long legs stretched towards Sarah as he lounged in his seat, a ray of sunlight across the length of his boots, bringing out a reddish tint in the supple leather.

"You are no doubt very curious about Zain Hassan bin Hamid, and so I'll enlighten you a little. His ways, *bint*, are not entirely those of his countrymen; his preferences are not always in line with other males of his tribe. That he gets away with being a little different in his attitudes is due to his toughness of character. Berbers admire this quality and expect it in a leader. A soft man would soon have trouble on his hands, and the tribe would break up and be dispersed into the cities, where all their fine, open-air qualities would be ruined. The people of the Beni Zain belong under the stars and the sun, in the wind and the rain – and it does rain in the desert, quite energetically. The Beni Zain are children of the elements, and it is the task of the Khalifa to keep them that way. He is their tamer and their keeper."

"The master who never relaxes his hold on his whip," said Sarah.

"But nonetheless an exciting and important task for a man to have." Sarah's escort gave her an intent look, all the more disturbing from those eyes whose colour could only be likened to the flame that sometimes burns in the heart of a fierce fire. Looking back at him Sarah could understand why he was in the employ of the Khalifa – this was a man who would stop at nothing to get his own way, and he probably had nerves of steel, and emotions to match them.

"Are you so certain, Miss Innocence, that this is still a game, that you are here on the Moroccan Express, on your way to what may prove to be your fate? *Mektub*, as we say in the desert. That we do nothing of our own volition, for it's written that we take a certain road at a certain moment in our lives. Think for a moment. Would you be here if the course of your life were still running along familiar lines whose direction you were in control of – you know, and I know, that suddenly there came a traumatic break and you were flung off your smooth course and confronted by an old road leading backwards, and a new road leading – ah, you catch your breath. You wonder if I make guesses, or a few enquiries about a young Englishwoman who answers an odd advertisement in a magazine."

"So – so you know about me." She felt resentful, as if he had torn aside a veil and left her totally insecure. Damn him! He was the kind who would be in the Khalifa's confidence; a sort of cool, confident *aide-de-camp* who vetted everyone who went in and out of the high lord's presence. Her green eyes shimmered in her face . . . that look he was giving her made her feel *naked*, and she hated him for it.

"Did you really think you would be taken at face value?" he asked, with a touch of scorn. "You're a little too good-looking to be in desperate need of employment so right away I sensed some other purpose in your application to be a companion. What is it, *bint*? Can't you face life without the bright tinsel wrapped around it? Is that why you're here – because you are running away? Everybody's pet doll who is afraid to be a woman?"

"You – you're as unfeeling as that iron track out there," she cried. "Furthermore, I wasn't everybody's pet doll –"

"Only that of a certain gentleman, eh?"

"You know everything, don't you?" Her fingernails dug into her bag and she felt she could have scratched out those blue eyes for seeing all that she was, a lost and lonely bit of a girl behind her façade of false confidence.

A friendless waif rather than a blasé woman of the world.

Gritting her teeth at him, she indicated her left leg. "You couldn't have known about this or I wouldn't be here, would I? How will you explain that to His Excellency, that you've brought all these miles a lame duck who hasn't just twisted her ankle but who will always be like this. I'm maimed, and I don't doubt that only perfection was to be put on the slave block for your master to choose from. What will you do now, for you've bungled the job, haven't you, mister high and mighty *aide-de-camp*?"

If Sarah expected to see him shaken she was disappointed, for he merely flicked his glance up and down her left leg, and he said lazily: "You have a run in your nylon stocking, *bint*. Are you so broke that you couldn't afford a new pair?"

"Go to the devil!" Sarah's eyes were a sheer apple-green in that moment, slanting in her white face above the delicate chiselling of her cheekbones. "Although, looking at you, it wouldn't surprise me if you're already well in league with him!"

"Kezam Zabayr added a rider that you had a rather indiscreet tongue, but he was so taken with your beauty that he decided your quick temper could be ignored –"

"Why, have you ways of dealing with that at Beni Zain?" she broke in, "as you deal with women who take lovers? Do you remove the tongues of your more out-spoken *kadins*?"

"In your case it might be an advantage." He abruptly leaned forward and Sarah actually felt the movement of his blue eyes over her features, like twin flames travelling her skin and leaving a trail of burning warmth – a *blush*, and she had almost forgotten how to blush during her years as a model, to whom the scrutiny of men becomes too commonplace to have much effect on the sensibilities.

But this was different – this was like an invasion of her privacy.

57

"We teach them," he said deliberately, "to know their places as women –"

"Under your heel, scared and submissive." Sarah glared at him, bristling like a small cat looking at a large one . . . a sleek tawny brute which had never known the softening influence of civilization but had lived always in the wilds of the desert. "If you think you can tame me, then you're in for a surprise. I'd fight you to the last spit and scratch!"

"Oh, I don't doubt it," he agreed. "But you aren't for me, are you, *bint*? You go to be looked over by a Khalifa."

"He won't choose me. I just told you – I'm maimed." Sarah flung up her chin and hated the word even as she used it. It was horrible, but it was only the truth – she had been beautiful, but now she was imperfect; she walked haltingly instead of being able to swing along with supple grace and freedom.

"I was watching you as you came out of the airport at Casablanca," he said, in that deep almost grating voice, with an inflection on certain words that made it startling that he spoke such faultless English – where had a barbarian learned it? Sarah stared at him across the compartment, held by his voice and his eyes. "I saw that you limped, Miss Innocence, but nonetheless you are here, are you not? Travelling to Beni Zain with me."

"You aren't the Khalifa," she said. "It's no skin off your nose if I happen to be lame – I'm not being put up for auction in front of you, am I?"

"Do you wish that you were?" he drawled. "Now there is a fascinating supposition – what would you do if I were the man who is to select a woman, from six candidates of every colour from gold to ivory; from warm brown to cool white? What would you do, *bint*? Scream or faint?"

"I think," she bit her lip, hiding its sudden tremor, "I think I'd jump out of this train –"

"Now that is a childish thing to say," he mocked.

"No man is worth a beautiful white body wasted beneath the sharp wheels of a speeding train. Who knows, you might enjoy being my *kadin*. There have been women who have enjoyed themselves in my desert tent."

"I don't doubt it," she rejoined, "but I haven't any ambition to join their ranks, for the dubious honour of being tamed to your hand. I'll take my chance with the Khalifa."

"You feel so confident that he'll pass you over?" The blue eyes raked her face. "You possess a charming face, and I'm sure you know it, though in the East we do say that beauty is only perfect when it is like the limpid pool set among the trees of the oasis, silent and utterly precious to the weary traveller."

"There you are then," she said. "That is what your Khalifa will look for in the woman he chooses for his sisters, a woman content to be seen but not heard."

"But you have opinions and you like to express them, eh?" He wore a smile, albeit an enigmatical one, as there came a sudden discreet knock on the door of the compartment.

"*Entrez,*" he called out.

The white-robed man who entered spoke not in French, which Sarah would have understood as she had taken the trouble to learn the language in which so much fashion was discussed, but he obviously used Arabic, and his manner towards her escort was decidedly deferential. Looking at his swarthy, hawkish face, Sarah realised that she had noticed several such men on the station platform, who had seemed to surge aboard the train in the wake of herself and the man who had literally yanked her into this compartment.

He replied in deep-throated Arabic to the tribesman who then inclined his head and backed out into the corridor.

"Mehmed is bringing us some luncheon. I imagine that

you must be feeling rather hungry?"

Sarah met the blue eyes in that equally swarthy and hawkish face, the lean lines of it almost ruthless in their definition. Heavens, could anything be more startling than those eyes in such a face!

"I am rather hungry," she admitted. "Who is that man?"

"Part of the retinue who travels with us to Beni Zain. In England you would probably call Mehmed a butler, except that this one is very efficient with a gun – don't forget, Miss Innocence, that this is the desert and anything might be hiding beyond that golden crest of sand or that high escarpment of primeval-looking rock."

He gestured beyond the window of the train, with the lean hand that carried an ancient ring stamped with a well-worn insignia. Sarah felt a deepening curiosity about him as she glanced towards the desert, like a great sandy pelt peeled from the back of a lion, where the very next moment a grove of petrified trees appeared, looking as if they had been carved from grey stone.

"It's strange," she said. "I expected the desert to be a rolling mass of golden sand, but it's more than that, isn't it? It's curiously alive with strange things, and ridged all over like an animal pelt. It lives and breathes, doesn't it? Like the sea."

"You are perceptive," he murmured, "for a young woman who has spent much of her time in and out of fashion salons. Pretty women are so often empty-headed, but you do a lot of thinking, don't you?"

"Oh, it's well known that men imagine you must look like a horse if you're halfway intelligent –"

"Horses aren't all that intelligent," he said, in the crisp voice of someone who knew. "They take a lot of training and can still prove feckless."

"Like pretty women, I suppose?" she shot at him, quivering inwardly as she thought of that awful moment when the Grey Lady had lost control on the Downs and galloped madly as if from her own shadow, to fling Sarah head-first at a great tree. Sarah knew she would never ride again. Her nerve was broken and she never wanted to sit in a saddle ever again.

She could feel the penetrating gaze of this tall, arrogant man of the desert who shared the confidence of Zain Hassan bin Hamid. He no doubt thought that his master should hire a woman of Berber blood and not waste his time on a pale-skinned creature like herself. Sarah tried to drag her eyes from that deep opening in his tunic, where the skin of his chest was no less dark than that of his face. He was a tawny devil, born of the sands, the winds, and the flaming desert sun.

Mehmed reappeared at that moment, carrying a food basket which when opened revealed a selection of cooked meats, some jars of pickles, a large flask of coffee, and several sorts of fruit. Sarah's escort said something to his manservant, who again withdrew from the compartment and left them to help themselves to the food and drink.

It was delicious, Sarah had to admit it to herself even as she took a sip at the hot, aromatic coffee.

"You believe in travelling in comfort," she remarked.

"When a train is available, but the story becomes a different one when a journey is made by camel and lunch is taken where a rock might offer some shade. Then this delectable cheese and pepper salad might be covered in sand grains and tiny flies."

"Ugh!" Sarah pulled a wry face as she accepted the carton of salad, in which was also boiled egg and beetroot cut into chunks. On a flap of bread she was handed a pair of crisp wings of partridge, and she settled herself in the corner of her seat to enjoy this unexpected picnic. Mmmm, the meat was cooked to perfection, and the contents of the salad were dressed with a mayonnaise from out of a dream. As she ate, with a frank and dainty greediness, Sarah cast

61

little looks at her host from beneath her lashes. A barbarian with a taste for excellent cuisine . . . a high placed member of the Khalifa's staff who believed in making the most of his position of trust.

"I am glad you aren't one of those women who picks and pecks at her food," he said, his firm teeth tearing at the partridge with an equal frankness of appetite. "One should always take advantage of the good things which Allah has provided for us. Life is to be lived, not looked at through the bars of convention and restraint. You like our Eastern provender, eh?"

"Well, it's hardly goat cheese and water," she replied. "You do yourself proud, don't you?"

"I would be a fool not to, *bint*, seeing that I am in such close touch with the Khalifa."

"What is a *bint*?" she asked. "You say it as if it might be a bit of an insult. I know you don't think much of me –"

"It means girl, Miss Innocence. Merely that and no more. You are a girl in many ways, are you not? Kezam Zebayr reported that you had not yet crossed the Rubicon."

"Crossed the –?" Sarah gazed at him wide-eyed, then it came to her what he meant and she blushed vividly. "You know everything, don't you? Every word I spoke at that interview has been reported to you for your vetting. Can't your master be bothered to do it himself? Is that too much trouble as well?"

"As well?" He held the flask poised above her coffee cup.

"Does he leave it to you to find girls for him?" Sarah became suddenly reckless, her annoyance with everything about this man rising up and overwhelming her. "As you very obviously aren't a eunuch, then I take it you are the one who does the procuring for him? Very obviously you wouldn't be allowed inside his *zenana*!"

The train sped on through the hot day, a shimmering vista beyond its windows that gave everything an unreal quality. Horribly real was the echo of Sarah's unguarded words and the deep twin blazes that came alive in the depths of those eyes that held all the ageless paganism of the desert which had bred him.

"It is just as well for you tha* you are a *naif bint*," he said, and there was at the edge of his words a razored, almost whispering quality, as of fine-honed steel slicing across a white throat. "Your adventure *risqué* has brought you into realms where not so long ago prisoners were fed to tigers, and decapitated heads leered on spikes from the walls of a despot's palace. Slave sales were public occasions, and lovely female captives were held to ransom. This is Barbary, where the last of the corsairs have their *kasbahs*, and care very little what goes on in the world beyond their own kingdoms."

"If you're thinking of getting ransom for me, then you'd get very little," she said defiantly. "I have nobody in England who cares enough to buy me back from a barbarian like you."

"Not even the English gentleman?"

"He least of all." She couldn't help glancing down at her weak ankle, and it all flooded back, the anger and the mortification. "I mean nothing to him, and he means even less to me."

"You are all alone, eh, with not a soul to care if you never appear again in the places where you were known? You have come all this way without informing a single friend?"

"I wasn't in a confiding mood – anyway, they'd have said I was crazy and asking for trouble –"

Sarah broke off, staring into the hard brown face of this stranger who looked as if he enjoyed trouble, especially the sort that would have been implicit in the warnings of other people.

A hand crept to her throat, where a pulse beat madly – and she had foolishly blurted out to him that not a single acquaintance had any idea that she was here in Morocco!

"I see it in your eyes, Miss Innocence, that you belatedly agree with what your friends would have said." His smile was a sardonic twist of the lips, and he leaned a little towards her, as if to enjoy all the more the sudden look of terror in her green eyes.

CHAPTER FOUR

Unable to bear his scrutiny, and what she knew he was seeing in her eyes, Sarah turned her head away and stared from the train window – and saw inescapably the miles of desert that surrounded them. She saw the ruthless blueness of the sky that was reflected in the eyes that still watched her . . . she could feel them. "A turbaned son of Satan!" Who had said that? Was it a hundred years ago, or only moments ago? It didn't matter when, for it was all too true. When he had leaned towards her she had felt the controlled devilment of the man – the alertness, the danger, the agility of some great sand leopard. His apparel added to the impression, that white tunic slashed at the brown chest, the black breeches and high boots laced with strips of leather.

"White ivory," she heard him say, "was what they called a white captive woman."

"You aren't frightening me!" Her defiant eyes flashed to his face. "That man who brought lunch – those other men, they know I'm here with you!"

"Of course they know." He drawled the words. "Will you have a little more of this excellent coffee? Arabian coffee, spiced as only we know how."

Her throat had gone so dry that she was badly in need of refreshment and didn't refuse the coffee when it was poured. But the cup shook slightly in her hand as she carried it to her lips, and she hated that giveaway sign of nervousness. It proved how insecure she felt in his presence; how unsure she was of his intentions. That she was lame in one foot didn't alter the fact that she was a female and an attractive one, and there was no denying the fact that she was very much in the hands of this man.

"Is that better? Is the throat less like a dry gulch where a sand cat crouches?"

He leaned back in his seat and took from a pocket of his breeches a leather folder that when opened was half filled with cheroots. Very slim, the length of cigars, and strong and dark as the devil eyebrows above his glinting eyes. His lean fingers played with a cheroot as he selected it, crackling the leaf.

"Slip off your jacket and be more comfortable," he drawled. "We have a few more hours of train travel ahead of us, and I am going to make myself at ease with a cheroot. You won't mind that I smoke?"

"Would it matter if I did mind?" From chills she had gone to a feeling of almost fainting heat, and it was a relief to peel off her jacket and feel a little cooler in her blouse of ivory corded silk, very nicely tailored and expensive. As a model she had had a weakness for good quality clothes and it was an indulgence which had depleted her bank balance and brought her – she bit her lip – into the clutches of this tall arrogant devil, the flame of a match almost at his fingertips as he lit his cheroot with deliberation.

He drew in the smoke and emitted it from his hawkish nostrils, and Sarah breathed it in, tangy and indefinably foreign, mingling with the aroma of Arabian coffee and creating a blend that she would never forget again . . . if she were ever lucky enough to escape from this *risqué* situation into which she had flown like a foolish butterfly. *Poor butterfly* . . . the words of that old-fashioned song ran through her mind. With no one to blame but herself for her predicament!

"Have some fruit," he drawled. "Those grapes look inviting and will cool your throat."

More for something to do than from any wish to eat anything more, Sarah broke off a few of the grapes from the bunch that reposed on a round of the flat, tasty bread.

"We call our bread *kesrah*," he said lazily. "It comes in handy as a plate – saves the washing-up."

Sarah flicked a look at him – so flagrantly male and sure of himself, and of what he intended to do with her.

"Women are like grapes," he went on, smoke drifting from his half-mocking lips. "If you take a bite before they are ripe, then you are sure to get a gripe."

"What a delightful piece of philosophy," she said, crunching one of the big grapes and finding it incredibly sweet. "It has to be your own, I feel sure of that."

"You begin to know me," he mocked. "Those grapes are almost the colour of your eyes – *fleur de nil* in the sunlight. I wonder what shade they are in the moonlight?"

"You are likely to go on wondering," she rejoined. "And please don't think that you have to pay me compliments – I feel much happier without them."

"Perhaps you mean that you feel safer." He smoked his cheroot in a lazy fashion, his robed head at rest against the back of his seat. "Picture it, the desert moon playing over the secretiveness of a walled garden, which we call a *zariba*, where the enchanter's nightshade grows and the fan-tailed raven flies. There is nothing more evocative than a Moorish garden, made for meditation, and for the saying of the things that in daylight have less meaning."

"I should have thought you preferred the freedom of the desert to the seclusion of a garden," she said, infusing a note of cool indifference into her voice. She didn't want it to show that his deep voice sent odd vibrations through her nervous system . . . she didn't like him one little bit, but there was a curious fascination about him. He struck her as being quite lawless . . . even unscrupulous in the way he took advantage of his position as *aide-de-camp*. There seemed to be two sides to him, a very educated one, and a frankly barbaric one. There was no knowing from one moment to the next which side would be shown to her.

"Let us say that when I am riding in the desert I would be

nowhere else, but when I am strolling in the coolness of a palm garden where the fountains make their cool music, the memory of the blistering desert is one I would forget. Every man has two sides to his nature. A light side and a dark one."

"What about women?" she asked. "Or are they objects of clear transparency to you?"

"As I said, *bint*, they are like the grape." He reached out his hand and plucked one from the bunch. "You see, it appears to be transparent, but hold it and there is no way of really judging how pippy it might be, or how tough to the bite the pretty skin might be, or even when it is sweet or sour. With a woman a man takes more chances than when he walks in a crowded *souk* where the thieves roam and the merchants offer gilt for gold."

"How very cynical you are! I thought that elemental people trusted in all sorts of myths and wonders, and had an almost superstitious awe of anything not fully under-stood – like a woman."

"Education is the enemy of elemental beliefs," he drawled. "I might have been a nicer man had it not been thought necessary to send me to school." He regarded his cheroot in a quizzical way. "I envy some of the tribesmen of the Beni Zain, for they have a far simpler outlook on life than I can ever have. I have to question the odd facts and fancies of life, whereas they accept them as good or bad. They marry very simply, have their families and their feuds, and go to paradise uncomplaining. Yes, let us say that I am less of a believer than they – perhaps it is in my blood. *Mektub*."

Sarah stared into his eyes and wondered if he had mixed blood. Was it usual for a Berber to have such astonishingly blue eyes – in contrast to his sunburned skin they were brilliant as sapphires.

"You could never be called dull." She spoke the words almost before she realised them, but they held a truth that couldn't be denied. Kezam Zabayr, in his well-tailored European clothes, had been far more the conventional type of Arab, but there was a distinct strangeness about this one. He was highly intelligent, but he was also untamed. He could never walk through European lounges without arousing speculation, and a certain consternation. There was a certain savagery about the man that was unmistakable . . . it would be like letting loose a leopard in a Regency drawing-room.

"Ah, now the lady pays me a compliment," he said, half-mockingly.

"I didn't mean it like that," she argued. "You know well enough that you're different from Kezam Zabayr and Mehmed."

"Because of my eyes, *bint*?" His words had become edged, reminding her again of a scimitar slicing through the air. "Blue eyes aren't unusual in the Barbary hills."

"No – it's your manner. You don't care a damn about anyone, do you?"

"I don't bow my head to anyone, if that is what you mean?"

"Yes – yes, that's what I mean. The pride of Lucifer, don't they call it?"

"Do they?" His eyes were arrogantly mocking as they dwelt on her slightly flushed face. "Lucifer was the right-hand man who fell from good grace, wasn't he, because of too much pride and ambition? Are you implying that I am in the same category and likely to fall from the Khalifa's good offices because of the same faults?"

"It's happened before, hasn't it? You don't strike me as a man who likes to be someone else's messenger."

"I believe procurer was the word you used, Miss Innocence."

Her flush deepened. "I – I don't always think before I speak –"

"Obviously. You rush in where angels fear to fly, and

now you find yourself on the Moroccan Express and deep in the heart of the Orient. You are not exactly a dull person yourself, *bint*."

"No —" She glanced from the train window and saw, indeed, how deep they were in the realms of burning sand, strange outcrops of rock, and the occasional oasis like a sudden miracle of green, where the black tents of the nomadic travellers were pitched in the shade of the tall palm trees.

"I could wish that I was less impulsive," she muttered. "I wasn't brought up to be heedless, but right now I'd change places with the dullest of suburban housewives. At least they know where they are, and the television news will assure them that the dangers are outside their cosy little nest."

"You would hate that," he drawled. "It would be like trapping a tiger moth in a milk bottle."

She shot a look at him and her green eyes were stormy. "I think you're getting a hell of a lot of pleasure out of seeing me writhe, like a moth on a hatpin. You saw me walk out of the airport and you could see I was lame – why couldn't you just send me packing instead of making me go through with this? Will it give you a kick to see me humiliated?"

"Why do you associate humiliation with your ankle?" he asked.

"Oh, don't pretend that men like girls who limp," she said heatedly. "I've had a sample of male reaction to a lame foot!"

"The Englishman, eh?" The cheroot stub was ground to shreds beneath his booted heel.

"I don't want to talk about him," she said contemptuously. "He's out of my life and good riddance. But it was being all mixed up after my accident that brought me here, and now I see how crazy I was to come on such a fool's errand. If you had an ounce of feeling you'd send me back to Casablanca – ”

"And what would you do there?" he asked. "You've admitted that you have very little money, and even making an appointment with the British Consulate would take time and you might be in Casablanca several days before the Consul could do anything to assist you."

"Oh, rub it in that I've been a headstrong fool," she drew herself even further into her corner, as if to retreat as far away as possible from his alien maleness. "You wouldn't have any pity for your own foot if it was caught in a trap."

"Self-pity is a sheer waste of time, and I have a philosophy which says that if you start a journey, finish it. If you begin a game of chance, then go through with it and see what turns up. Come, would you not remain forever curious about the outcome if you turned back now?"

"I know the outcome in advance," Sarah muttered, seeing again in her mind's eye the way Peter Jameson had retreated from her bedside when he had learned that she was maimed.

"All right, you know it." The hard shoulders lifted the tunic in a shrug. "You were told that you would be given the money to return home if you were not found – suitable. Think about the money, *bint*. It was that you came for, was it not?"

She flinched, for he had a way of hitting a nerve and making her feel very mercenary. "Well, it takes an opportunist to know another," she said. "You hate this whole business, yet you're a party to it – because you are well rewarded, I expect."

"With shekels or *kadins*?" he mocked. "Has it not occurred to you that the Khalifa might reward me with the girl of the green eyes and the red-gold hair?"

Sarah gave him a petrified look, seeing the pagan eyes and the brows that merged in a dark line above the formidable nose. She saw the hint of sensuous savagery in his mouth, and the way the *kibr* and the tight black breeches seemed to emphasize his lean strength and hard grace of body and limb.

Her face whitened until only her green eyes showed any colour, and the tiny mole on the pure line of her jaw. She swore to herself that she wouldn't shrink, faint, or burst into tears. The truth was that she felt like screaming the train to a halt.

This was the East, where these men made their own laws, and there was in that lounging male body a kind of arrogance that she couldn't help but associate with a lawless and savage animal. Had he had it in mind from the moment she emerged from the airport, to have her for himself?

Even as the thought ran riot in her brain, she leapt to her feet and looked round wildly for the alarm cord that would stop the train if she could manage to pull it.

But he was as swiftly on his feet, and even as she lurched with the motion of the train he caught hold of her and held her struggling in his arms.

There clung to him the woodsmoke of coffee fires, the aroma of strong tobacco, the tang of leather and horses. An indescribable blending of male essences, strange and inescapable as his arms about her frightened body.

"I think not," he snarled softly. "This train will not be stopping until it reaches Beni Zain."

And lifting her, he tossed her back into the corner from which she had sprung, and she lay there, out of breath, and filled with a mixture of fury and pure fright. Her hair had come loose from its bun and it clouded about her white face, filled with tiny red lights like danger signals.

He stood over her, swaying in time with the train, booted legs planted wide. Sarah felt the hammering of her heartbeats and knew that she had fallen into the hands of a man who was quite merciless. It would be useless to plead with him, and she still had a few fragments of pride left in her shaken body.

"Go to hell," she said, and was pleased that she managed

72

to get the words out so concisely.

"Yes," he rejoined, "I can take you there, *bint*, but it's written that a man goes alone to paradise."

"Paradise!" She gave him a scornful look. "I'd sooner take poison!"

He bowed sardonically when she said that, and sat down directly beneath the space in the wall where the alarm cord was situated. She saw this and curled her lip at him, then she turned her eyes away from him and gazed in a blind panic at the rolling sea of sands beyond the windows of the train.

What if she wrenched open the door and threw herself out, daring those thundering wheels that took her further each moment into the wilds where a woman was no more than an object for a man's pleasure! She gazed fascinated at the shimmering scene . . . aeons of sands that mesmerised like the depthless ocean.

"I shouldn't," said a voice, breaking into her thoughts like a stone thrown into a pool. "The velocity of the train would throw you under the wheels, not beyond them, and virtue was never worth a sacrifice that painful."

He was right, of course . . . damn him! Sarah closed her eyes and leaned her head against the padded seat; she listened to the rhythm of the wheels . . . come to me . . . come to me, they seemed to say, and a slow shiver went all through her slim body.

Come to me . . . come . . . until she found escape by falling off to sleep, curled into a corner like a small, lost cat.

Sarah awoke abruptly, still half dazed, to find herself being enveloped in a great cloak. Even as a protest cried through her and reached her lips, a fold of the cloak was flung over her face and she was carried bodily from the compartment, along the corridor, and out upon the platform. The arms that bound her within the folds of the cloak were as strong as leather cords and she was quite helpless as she was carried from the station, though she could hear the throaty murmur of several male voices, and then another sound like a chorus of gurgling groans.

The fold of cloth was removed from her face and she was confronted by the sight of about a dozen camels being urged to their feet from where they had been lounging in the shade of a white wall. They were in assorted shades of buff and brown, with serpentine necks and scornful lips drawn back from fierce-looking teeth. And all the time they groaned as they rose on their long legs, their high-placed saddles hung with bobbles and fringes in bright colours.

The scene for Sarah was like something out of a Moorish legend . . . was it real, or was she still asleep and dreaming?

"We travel the rest of the way by camel back." The fierce blue eyes looked down into hers. "I can see that you are ready with your objections, but they will be a waste of breath."

"I – I've never been on a camel in my life!" she gasped, and was aware of those other robed men standing around and watching intently as she argued with their chief.

"You will travel in the *haudaj*." He gestured at a creamy-beige-coated camel with a tent-like structure attached to its saddle; the curtained camel-seat in which travelled the women of a desert retinue.

"Oh no – " Sarah began to struggle within the confines of the cloak and her green eyes shot sparks of defiance up into the hard-boned face of the man who held her. "I'm not some damned harem favourite, being escorted across the sands to your tent! I won't do it! I won't!"

"Would you have gone on horseback if I had ordered horses instead of camels?" he taunted, and as he spoke Sarah heard the sound of the Moroccan Express starting up and preparing to continue its journey to Fez or Safi,

74

or one of the other cities where at least a layer of civilized living lay over the aromatic depths of Arabian life.

Here was where civilization left off, and looking wildly around her Sarah saw late afternoon sun shimmering on the long ridges of the sand dunes that stretched away towards the dusky gold horizon.

"I came with you because I thought you were taking me to the castle of the Khalifa, but that isn't your intention at all, is it?" Her left hand dragged its way out of the cloak and was reaching for his lean jaw when his fingers caught her by the wrist and she felt his grip like a vice.

"What is my intention, little fool?" he growled. "To take you crumpled and terrified to some hideaway of my own in the depth of the desert? My foolish *bint,* I am not so desperate for a woman that I need do such a thing, as if your white skin, your emerald eyes, and your red hair had gone like strong wine to my weak head. What do you take me for? Some reckless young lance who aims himself at the first piece of fruit on the tree? Look well at me, Miss Innocence. Do I look a mere boy?"

Her eyes raced over his face, which set against that coppery gold sky was like a mask etched upon a Byzantine frieze. Powerful, brooding, lit strangely by those intense blue eyes.

Reluctantly she shook her head and realised that she had behaved like a panicky fool.

The edge of his teeth showed in a brief smile. "You have been reading too many novels about headstrong heroines and love-hungry sheiks," he drawled. "My men and I are taking you to the *kasbah* in the far hills of Beni Zain. This is only the outskirts of the region, but the Khalifa's power is too widespread, and his temper too well known, for any one of his men to ride off with a woman meant for his appraisal, and possible appreciation. Now will you be docile and ride in the *haudaj*? I assure you it is far more comfortable than it probably looks."

"I – I seem to have no choice," she said. "I have your word that we are bound for the *kasbah*?"

"My solemn word," he said mockingly. "It seems that you have got it into your head that the Khalifa is less to be feared than his – what was it you called me? – *aide-de-camp*. I hope you are not in for a big surprise."

"I hope so as well," she rejoined. "But at least he has to be a gentleman, which you certainly aren't, bundling me up in your cloak and carrying me off the train like so much laundry!"

"I didn't wish certain of the other passengers to see you." He said it quite deliberately. "I thought it better not to arouse anyone's curiosity about a red-haired woman being escorted from the Moroccan Express by a dozen tribesmen of the Beni Zain. What the eye doesn't see, the mind doesn't ponder. You comprehend?"

"In a manner of speaking." She looked directly into his eyes. "I take it these other women have gone openly to the *kasbah* of your Khalifa, yet you are making a big secret of my presence in Beni Zain. Can you wonder that I feel – suspicious?"

"Those other women are not as you!" He said it arrogantly, and beckoned to one of his men, who took the creamy-beige camel by its reins and brought it forward, the *haudaj* swaying on its humped back. Sarah stared at the animal and the curtained saddle seat – it looked precarious placed up there and despite his assurances not too comfortable.

Abruptly, as the animal was urged into a kneeling position, the cloak was withdrawn from her and she was dropped to her feet. "Come." He took her by the wrist and led her to the camel, who turned its head and watched with a sulky eye embedded in enormous lashes as she was assisted into the seat, which was of scarlet leather hung with tassels, and the curtains were slowly drawn around her.

"It will feel a little like being on the water." There was a

76

sardonic note in the deep voice a moment before the lean hand was withdrawn, and she was left to clutch at the saddle as the camel towered to its feet and she was high in the air, pulling open the curtain again and looking down aghast at the shimmering sea of sand all around her. Her escort had mounted a camel near her own and he had hold of both sets of reins. When he caught her looking out of the curtains of the *haudaj*, he broke into a smile that made his teeth a white bar against his tanned skin.

"You will be sea-sick if you look downwards as we ride," he called out to her, and then he must have repeated his words in Arabic, for his men burst into laughter, a rich and throaty sound mingling with the jingle of harness and the groans of the camels as the party set off at a comfortable trot which to Sarah felt exactly like the pitching and swaying of a cockleshell boat on a wavy sea.

It was all too fantastic for reality, and yet it was real, for she could feel the desert wind in her face, and across the sky was spreading a great pool of colour, as if many oriental dyes had run together to form those great splashes of gold and lavender, of purest green and apricot, of amethyst and smoky pink.

It was sheer, indescribable beauty, of a depth and meaning that went beyond the glossy descriptions of the East that were found in travelogues.

There was a golden glamour to it all, a wild and spicy tang to the air, and a tingling awareness in Sarah's veins of mystery and a sense of danger which had not diminished when the blue-eyed Berber had said that they were bound for the Khalifa's residence. There he sat at his arrogant ease on the hump of his camel, one leg hooked casually around a part of the saddle, handling his mount and hers with no apparent difficulty.

Sarah just didn't trust him . . . she felt instinctively that he was playing some kind of a game with her, and there was absolutely nothing she could do about it. Despite her struggles and her protests, here she was in the middle of the desert, seated in a *haudaj* like some captive bird in a cage.

She felt the flat-footed motion of her camel, and heard without understanding the throaty conversation of the men who formed a kind of guard of honour around her and the man in command of them. They were clad in white, but over his tunic and breeches he wore a black and floating *burnous*, the dark cloth drawn across his face and revealing only his eyes. He looked more than ever a man to be feared, the dark visor he had drawn across his mouth and nose giving him the sinister look of a desert eagle, his eyes moving back and forth across the great ridges of sand as if he might swoop down on the first living thing that moved across his line of vision.

Sarah clutched the pommel of her saddle and felt the tension in her gripping fingers. The long, loping stride of the camels took them ever deeper into the heart of the desert, and here among the eternal sands very little had really changed since the days when Cain had slain his brother . . . since the veiled men of the Rif had come swooping down on the caravans that carried spices and tea, and pet cats and women wrapped in silken rugs . . . since a certain rare Englishman had led an Arab revolt against the Turks.

Sarah's heart beat with a strange, apprehensive excitement . . . when her surgeon had suggested that she take a holiday, he had meant a restful and relaxing one on the sands of a seaside resort – what would he say, or anyone who had known her as a chic young model, if they could see her right now, perched up high like this, the only female among a band of lawless-looking Berbers, hawk-faced and robed to their piercing eyes.

She was unsure how many miles they travelled on that first lap across the sands, but the sun had gone down in flames, and the huge stars had come alight in the sky

78

when with a motion of his hand her escort brought the men and camels to a halt. Towering to the left of where they halted was a great escarpment of rock, rising into the sky like an ancient, petrified fortress with jagged turrets and broken bastions.

Again with a chorus of grunts and groans the camels were brought to their knees and the men alighted. Sarah's camel was urged more slowly into a kneeling position, and even before she prepared to slide to the ground she felt the cramp in her left foot and knew that she was going to stumble badly.

Arms caught hold of her and she was held a moment, wincing with the pain that still came as a residue of the agony she had suffered at first, before the torn and broken tendons began to heal. The pain ran up into the calf of her leg and she gave a shudder. The hands holding her must have felt it, for instantly he knelt and taking hold of her leg he began to massage the cramped muscle.

"Don't – " she started to say, annoyed by the weakness of her leg, and the startling intimacy of those hardened hands on her person.

"The aching won't go without help," he said curtly, "so stop jibbing like a nervous filly."

With firm movements of his lean fingers he gradually eased away the cramp and when Sarah was able to put her foot to the ground he rose to his feet, the *burnous* billowing around him like a great black wing.

"Don't be such a proud little fool," he said, still speaking with great curtness. "In the desert we look after each other because it's a dangerous place in which to be hurt or ill. It's a very ruthless place, *bint*. A garden of Allah and hell. Come, the men will light the coffee fires and prepare a meal, for this is where we rest for a few hours."

Sarah found when she moved that he still had his fingers tightly locked about her wrist; her impulse was to jerk away from him, for he was unutterably disturbing in his

79

black robes, towering above her in the radiant starlight. She wasn't exactly short herself, but this man wasn't only tall but he walked with a kind of hauteur that added to his impressive height. In all his actions he made her feel very much a girl in his absolute charge, and there was no doubt that the members of his entourage looked upon him as a man of importance.

Sarah felt his grip upon her and realised that there was nothing she could do but fall in with his wishes. She had seen that he could evoke obedience from his hawkish servants with a slight lift of his eyebrows, and she felt too bone-jolted and weary to fight with him right now.

"I – I wonder if it would be possible for me to – to have a wash?" she asked, a rather desperate little note in her voice. "I know water is in short supply in the desert, but I saw that one of the camels was carrying a large water-bag."

He glanced down at her and his eyes flicked her face, which looked pale and strained in the milky dazzle of the huge stars . . . stars which seemed to hang incredibly close to the sand dunes.

"In short supply or not, I would be a brute, eh, to refuse you the second most valued thing in your life . . . at the moment." He moved at her side with the lean and lethal grace of a leopard, and his slight smile didn't soften the dangerous mouth with the hard white teeth that would have no liking for soft, sweet things. His glance ran from her eyes to her lips, from her throat to her ankles. The wind across the desert spaces caught at her hair and her clothes. She felt dazed and untidy, and her eyes pleaded even if she didn't want them to do so.

"You will?" She hardly dared to believe that he could be magnanimous enough to let her waste any of their precious water. "Oh, I'd be so grateful – !"

"Don't be too grateful," he drawled. "A barbarian like me is likely to get the wrong idea."

As he spoke he beckoned one of his men and spoke

to him for several minutes, while Sarah stood and watched the changing expressions on the tribesmen's face, the look of politeness merging into a stare of wonderment. Then he salaamed and walked to where the various bundles had been removed from the camels and piled on the ground.

"Daylis will arrange that you have privacy for your wash by putting up a tent and finding you some sort of a wash-bowl. It will all be rather primitive, but you appreciate that this is unavoidable in the circumstances."

Sarah knew that he was being sardonic, but she was too grateful to care if Daylis provided her with a soup tureen to bathe in so long as she felt water against her skin and could have a change of clothing.

"I shall need my suitcase," she said. "It's very good of you to arrange this for me."

"Good I am not," he drawled, "but I do appreciate that you are a female and that this is the first time you have journeyed in the heat and sand of the desert. You have a desperate need to feel clean. I understand, though of course my men find it rather amazing. We wear these voluminous robes and they keep out much of the grit that the desert wind carries, and they also provide a certain ventilation when they blow about. We are used to the conditions of these vast spaces of sand and our skins become almost as tanned as leather, but your skin is another matter."

She caught the glint of his teeth, and felt his glance on her neck in the opening of her shirt. He knew there were sand grains rubbing against her skin, feeling as big as grits caught as they were between the silk of her slip and her body. She bit her lip, for it struck her as intensely personal that this tall Berber should be so aware of her feminine requirements . . . up until now he hadn't struck her as being much of a ladies' man, but suddenly she realised that his religion permitted him three wives and as many *kadins* as he could afford. In an instant she was intensely aware of the masculinity of the man, intensified by his understanding of her need to wash away those clinging grains of sand.

Smoke arose in the air from the coffee fires, and there was a distinct sound of the wind across the desert which had grown very cool now that night had fallen. High above the encampment rose those petrified sand towers, and it was at the foot of them that Daylis pitched her bathing tent.

When she entered she found that a lamp had been lit and hung upon the tent pole. A few goatskin rugs had been laid upon the floor, and upon one of these stood a steaming bowl of water. It wasn't a large bowl, but it was big enough, and Sarah saw her suitcase on a little stool. With a sigh of pleasure she opened her case and took out fresh clothing, her soap, sponge and towel, and discarding any lingering shreds of prudery she quickly stripped and stepped into the bowl.

Even if it was but a sponge down, it was most refreshing, and she had no fears of her silhouette being seen, for the walls of the tent were of black woven wool and she felt as reasonably secure as she was able, in the encampment of a dozen desert tribesmen. The tent had a spicy, primitive smell that wasn't in the least unpleasant, and standing on one of the goatskin rugs Sarah towelled herself down, her toes tickled by the long hair of the rug. Feeling clean and fresh, she dressed in a pair of slacks and a roll-neck sweater in jade-green jersey. She brushed her hair and pinned it back in a classic chignon, which she had learned to do without the aid of a mirror, a good style for modelling, and also one that suited her face with its high cheekbones and tapering jawline.

Sarah smiled a little to herself, for she realised the incongruity of a fashionable young woman in a goat-hair tent in the desert, and she also felt the quickening of hunger when she stepped outside and caught the aroma of lamb kidneys and sausages being fried in large pans on the open brushwood fires. The long-spouted coffee pots stood ready in the warm ashes at the edge of the fires, and some of the men were feeding the camels before settling down to their own supper.

She glanced around for that extra tall figure, and to her surprise saw him emerging from a tent similar to her own. She stared, for his head-cloth was off and he wore a dark kaftan over loose trousers that tapered off into flat-heeled leather slippers. He looked at once more approachable, and at the same time more disturbing. As he strolled her way in the glow of the fires he had the relaxed air of a man totally at one with his environment, and as he drew nearer she saw how black was his close-cut hair, and it had the gleam of hair which had been well wetted and slicked back with a comb.

So he, too, had indulged in a sponge bath, despite his assertion that men of the desert grew used to being in the saddle for long hours and didn't pamper themselves.

Sarah felt a little smile forming on her mouth . . . this educated barbarian could probably out do his fellow tribesmen in living rough and riding hard, but right now he had a woman in his camp and he wasn't going to smell of sweat and camel when he sat down to supper with her.

Her smile quivered on lips both nervous and knowing. "I must say I thoroughly enjoyed my wash – did you?"

He gave a sardonic inclination of his dark head. "It is only *politesse du coeur* to act the gentleman upon occasion," he drawled. "Especially when one is with a Nazrana, who judges a man by how many baths he takes rather than how many prayers he says."

"That isn't true," she exclaimed. "The thing I hate most in the world is a dirty mind, and all the soap and water in the world won't wash that out."

"You think I have a dirty mind – with regard to you, *bint*?" He stood there in the firelight, wearing the un-

83

changing garments of the desert, which allowed such freedom of movement for these men who were so lean, hard and agile. Sarah tensed and was aware of how leopard-quick he would be in pursuit of game . . . and right now she was his game.

"I think you have a devious mind," she said. "Women are male sport, aren't they?"

"Upon occasion," he admitted. "Though I have been known to enjoy the falcon on my wrist as much as I might enjoy a woman in my arms. Right now I wish to enjoy my supper, so we shall be seated so that Mehmed can serve us. I hope you like a mixed fry-up, with sliced potatoes and small onions in the pan? My men and I are partial, and with hot coffee, and the tang of woodsmoke, it can be better than a king's feast – or a woman's favours."

He indicated that Sarah be seated on the carpet which had been unrolled within the glow of one of the fires, and when she had curled down, glad that she had thought to wear a pair of slacks, he lounged beside her and they were both given large enamel plates of the smoking food, with slices of *kesrah*, and mugs of aromatic coffee.

His eyes flicked her trousers. "I hope you feel like one of the boys," he said drily. "Yes, I fear you will have to eat with your fingers, but it's part of the fun."

"I don't mind," she assured him, and proceeded to tuck into the food with the appetite of a young navvy, chewing the sausages and kidneys from her fingers, and mopping up oniony gravy with the tasty bread. The sliced potatoes had been crisped to perfection, and the coffee was rich and smoky.

Was any of it real . . . that ink-blue sky of great shining stars, those looming crests of sand painted with shadows, those hammered profiles in the lift and fall of the flames, as detailed as if shaped from copper? She studied her own hand shining with grease, and glanced up swiftly into a pair of eyes that glinted like the wing-feathers of the kingfisher bird. The leaping flames cast their shadows over a face that was more vital than any other face she had ever seen.

"*Mère de Dieu!*" he murmured. "You know how to eat, but where do you put it all?" He tossed a chunk of meat in through his lips and chewed it. "*Une fausse maigre,*" she heard him drawl into his coffee mug.

Thin but shapely! He had spoke in French because he assumed that she didn't understand him, and Sarah was about to let him know that she did know the language when a whisper of caution made her hold her tongue. It might prove useful to let him think that she didn't understand French, which he spoke as faultlessly as he spoke English . . . this barbaric-looking man of the desert who might, or might not, be taking her to his master, Zain Hassan bin Hamid.

She looked up at the sky and never in her life had she seen so many stars . . . one might stand on that fortress of rock and pluck a star for a souvenir. Then she caught her breath as one of them broke loose and began to fall through the sky. "That is a soul tossed into purgatory," said the man at her side. "Another Lucifer, perhaps."

"Fallen from grace because of too much ambition," she said, catching the irony in his smile. "Heroes and gods are not immune, are they?"

"Nor are women," he said meaningly. "Look what you have risked, *bint,* because an advertisement stated that it was a gentleman of means who required a companion."

"You enjoy thinking of me as a mercenary woman, don't you?" She cupped her coffee mug in her hands, and the flickers of firelight were in her eyes as she looked at him. "It might interest you to know that my operations were expensive and when I came out of the clinic I had only a few pounds in the bank and little prospect of taking up my career again. I was finished as a model and – and nothing seemed to matter any more."

"Your rich gentleman no longer wanted you, eh?"

"I couldn't have cared less about him, but there's no fun in being out of work and – all right, I came here because there was a bit of money in it." She took a deep gulp of coffee. "I'm no angel, and you're certainly no saint, so don't sit in judgement on me!"

"Is that what I'm doing?" He lounged on his elbow, lazily at his ease after a good meal. Mehmed came to his side and proffered a box of cigars and he selected one with deliberation and had it lit for him from a burning stick which his manservant held. The leaping light of the flame played over his features, and then the smoke as he murmured a word of thanks and Mehmed bowed and withdrew.

"You know you are," she said. "You look at me as if – as if I have two faces and you're trying to get under my skin. Are you afraid your Khalifa might like me, and you think I'm not good enough for his sisters?"

The hard shoulders lifted the dark material of the kaftan and cigar smoke wreathed about his eyes giving them a veiled look. "Men can be deceived by a face, *bint*. The female voice can drip honey even as the slim hand curls around the hilt of a knife. It is never easy for a desert chief to trust people, for he can never tell if a serpent has been planted in his bosom."

Sarah stared at him and thought how strangely he spoke.

"Does he trust you?" she just had to ask.

"It is very hard to tell." The blue eyes brooded through the smoke. "Zain Hassan bin Hamid can never be sure if there is some plot afoot to dispose of him, or assassinate him. The blood in desert veins runs hot and strong and it can be readily aroused to hate – or love. Beni Zain is a large province and there are certain factions who would like to control it, but so far the present Khalifa retains his power and his control over his people. He is no tyrant, if that is what you are thinking, Miss Innocence."

The firm teeth gripped the dark cigar, and the eyes above the dominant nose held a glint of faintly chagrined amusement. "Let it be admitted that he trusts very few men, or women. It is the way of a tribal chief. Such a man cannot afford to be a trusting fool, for the desert is a vast place and the laws that can be enforced in cities are so much dust on the desert wind. It takes strength, and a certain ruthlessness, to be paramount chief of a large clan – if the Khalifa takes a second wife he must be sure that she is not part of a plot to dispose of him in the one place where most men are vulnerable – the bedroom."

"Is that possible?" Sarah looked aghast, and felt even more aware of the primitive forces of the desert. "What about – love?"

"Love!" He flicked ash with a fierce movement of his wrist. "It comes, if one is lucky, but more often in high places a woman's motive is mercenary, or political. Zain Hassan must marry again in due course, in order to have a son to take his place. It would be better for the safety of his skin and his tribe if the woman was mercenary."

"How cynical that sounds! How cold and calculating." Sarah felt a strange stab of pity for this man she was yet to meet.

"Are you still a romantic?" he mocked. "In spite of the English gentleman?"

"I – I was hurt because I believed he was sincere," she retorted. "And don't keep throwing him in my face; why do you do it – to be cruel?"

"Perhaps." His eyes narrowed as they raked over her face. "Are you looking for love in this land of singing silences?"

"No!" Her eyes were dilated, green as jade, and her mouth was tormented against the whiteness of her skin . . . she tried to wrench her gaze from his, but it held her as securely as a grip on her person; pinned her as a frightened moth to a blue-edged flame.

87

"You have hair the coppery-gold of a gold hawk's wing," he said, "and you need never wear jewels with eyes such as yours."

In the silence that hung between them at the conclusion of his startling words, Sarah heard the wailing music of a desert mandolin, and the deep-throated grunts of the kneeling camels. Sparks flew into the air from the fires, and the wind chased the sand around that immense escarpment of rock beneath which they were camped.

The moment brewed a quick panic in her, and then she made her eyes as coldly green as she possibly could.

"I can do without your compliments," she said. "Keep them for your dancing girls!"

"Not one of my dancing girls has fire in her hair, and in her veins," he said mockingly. "Not one of them has a pair of jades for a pair of eyes."

"I – I'm not staying here to listen to you –" She half rose to her knees, and then fell back at the formidable look that took possession of his face, making it look as hard and cruel as if cast in bronze, with not a tender feeling or a vulnerable emotion to ever soften him.

"Where will you go to get away from me?" he taunted her. "I could run you down, let alone ride you down, and if you have any crazy ideas about creeping off in the night, then I'll dispel them for you right now. You will sleep here at the fireside, close to my hand, and if you even turn over I shall hear you. Like sand cats we men of the desert sleep with an ear and an eye ever on the alert –"

"If you fondly imagine," she broke in, "that I'm going to sleep with you –"

"*Ma chère bint*, I said nothing of the sort." He put back his dark head and let forth a deep burst of laughter. "Who has the dirty mind, I wonder? You, I think."

"Oh – you're detestable!" Sarah glared at him, her eyes as green as a cat in a temper. "You take a delight in being mean to me!"

"I am merely safeguarding you for the Khalifa," he mocked. "He might have my hide if I allowed you to wander off into the desert, where anything might happen to you. Wild cats lurk among the rocks, not to mention wild men, to whom you would be a choice bone tossed among dogs. Do I make myself clear?"

"As crystal," she snapped. "What do you call yourself – a tame man, by any chance?"

"What do you call me?" He regarded her through his cigar smoke, with eyes that enjoyed her discomfiture, and yet held a lurking glint of curiosity. "I mean, apart from a procurer and an opportunist? Do you imagine that in the deep depths of the night I am going to ravish you – be the taster of the Khalifa's piece of English delight in case you should set his regal blood alight?"

"Go to –"

"Tell me once more to go there," he cut in, "and I shall teach you the meaning of the word."

"I know it," she flung back at him. "Where do you think I was when a damn horse flung me against a tree and crushed my foot? Do you think I was having tea at the Ritz when the doctors worked over me, and I lay in the dark knowing I'd limp for the rest of my life? It wouldn't have mattered so much if it hadn't been something that affected my career – I worked as hard as hell to get to the top of my profession, and then in a moment it was all gone, a-and I could have killed that brute of a horse!"

Her face was utterly white, and her eyes were a sheer blazing emerald. All the colour from her face seemed drawn into her vivid hair, and all at once a hard brown hand reached out and she wouldn't have shrunk away had he smacked her, but he merely touched her cheek, and from that she jerked away as if burned.

It was about half an hour later that Mehmed brought a huge rug to the fireside, a great soft covering of wolfskins sewn together. Part of it was laid over Sarah, while her Berber escort covered himself with the other half. She lay there tensely, aware of him with every separate nerve in her body ... she lay in the desert with a barbarian, folded up in a wolfskin to which clung an aroma of smoke, leather and spices.

"Go to sleep," he ordered her. "Some time tomorrow we shall reach the *kasbah* of Beni Zain and I don't want a weary woman on my hands, one who has lain awake in skittish fear of being ravished. I have never had to use force on any woman, and I'm not going to start with you, *bint*. Relax, close your eyes, or even count the stars if it will help, but do stop lying there so rigidly. *Rigor mortis* will set in if you aren't careful!"

For some reason – damn him – that amused her and she had to stuff a corner of her handkerchief into her mouth in order to stifle the nervous laugh that fluttered in her throat. Sleep, he said, as if every night of her life she was used to sharing wolfskins with a lean, long-legged Berber whose way of life was totally alien to all she had ever known.

Around her in the night was a low medley of strange sounds – the deep mutter of male voices, the grumbling of tethered camels, some of whom still munched their supper. Their neck bells made a music to which Sarah lay and listened, for she dared not listen to the breathing of the man who lay only inches from herself. She hardly dared to stir, for then he would be aware of her ... as a woman of another land ... an alien source whose skin, hair and eyes were different from those of the women who usually shared a rug with him, beneath the stars of the desert sky.

She wanted to sleep and yet she was afraid to fall asleep ... in case she awoke to find his arms around her, at the mercy of that hard and dangerous mouth that said things that left an unforgivable sting in their wake.

She fought to keep the weariness at bay, but it had been

a long, strange, active day, and she finally drifted off within the warmth of the wolfskins, only a few inches separating her from a man she barely knew . . . a man with the most lawless eyes she had ever looked into.

CHAPTER FIVE

Stone piled on stone, leaf hung upon leaf, rising up in a lordly, sand-coloured stack to the very skies and capped by roofs at all sorts of levels, some flat and others turreted, with crenellations that let in the hot sun.

It could well have been an ogre's castle, house of the enchanter, where strange things went on behind those thick walls crusted by sandstone and leaf-mould, and overlaid by ample creepers that clung to the stone like green serpents.

A place of power and torment, and dark desires aroused by harem beauties.

The *kasbah* of Zain Hassan bin Hamid, high lord of Beni Zain, chief of this vast region, the unknown devil who had played every game in the book of love and out of sheer politics had decided to see what an advertisement in an English magazine would bring to his divan. It could happen nowhere else but in this fabled place, Sarah told herself. Here where time had stood still, and a single man could command a great tribe and have each one at his beck and call.

A camel had brought her to Beni Zain, but she felt breathless, as if she had been wafted here on a magic carpet and brought to earth with hardly a ripple. She looked about her at the immense courtyard where she stood with her escort ... so he hadn't lied. Like all the others he was under the thumb of the Khalifa and for all his arrogance a mere subject like Mehmed and the other men.

She glanced at him and he might have been carved from palmwood, so powerful to look at in his great dark cloak, a corner of which was flung over his shoulder. He had an indisputable air of masculine command, yet here at the *kasbah* he was but a servant who had carried out his orders and would shortly leave her in the hands of other people ... strangers.

Feeling her eyes on his profile, he looked at her, and his eyes held a cool, almost dismissive look. *"Fait accompli,"* he murmured. "And you thought I had other ideas, eh?"

She pushed at a silky strand of hair which the desert wind had blown across her face, and desperately hoped that her colour hadn't risen. He wasn't exactly kind, but he had protected her in his own way, and she knew him just a little. "Oh, don't leave me," she wanted to say. "I'm scared out of my wits, and I know that any moment you're going to stride away and not look back at the little fool you have brought here."

She bit back the words ... as if he would care, one way or the other, what became of her! He had performed the task allotted to him and now he would go off and relax with the honey-coloured girls of his own race.

"There's no need to look as if your head is going on the block," he jibed. "They'll put all of you on the slave block, from your ankles to your flaming hair, and you asked for it, didn't you, *bint*?"

"I didn't ask to keep having it rubbed in that I've been an idiot," she exclaimed. "What will happen now? Will someone else take charge of me?"

"Yes. You will be taken to the *serayi* and will be given a female servant. You are trembling, eh?" With a slight flick of his wrist he had his riding-whip curled about her waist, and she gave a gasp at the trick, and felt him standing suddenly closer to her, looking down into her eyes and stunning her with the blueness of his own. If she never saw him again after today, the memory of his eyes would stay with her. In that face which the sun had tanned so deeply they were incredibly startling, and even rather beautiful.

"Don't wrench away or the leather will cut you," he

drawled. "Who knows, the Khalifa might dismiss you, and then I might put in a bid for the green-eyed Nazrana."

"You can't do that," she gasped, feeling the bite of the whip through the silk of her shirt. "It isn't in the agreement. If I'm not wanted, I'm to be sent home – they promised that!"

"At the kernel of every promise there is always a little doubt, like a fragment of shell that clings to the broken nut."

"What do you mean by that?" she demanded.

"My meaning shouldn't be that hard for you to grasp, Miss Innocence. Isn't it sticking in your teeth right now, the knowledge that you have come all this way without letting anyone know your whereabouts?"

"You mean – I could be kept here against my will?"

"It has happened to others, and everything that happens has a way of repeating itself." His smile grew infinitely mocking. "Think of the places in North Africa where a good price could be fetched for a white woman. It's true that not all my fellow tribesmen find a white skin to their liking, but you are young, nubile, and for a while longer there will be a silken sheen to your red hair."

She gazed up at him, horrified by the meaning in his words. Implicit in them was a terrible truth she had not fully realized until this moment. European girls did find their way into terrible vice dens in the Middle East, some of them willing victims, but others forced into the rackets by unscrupulous men who made love to them and then sold them into the pleasure houses.

"Tremble, *bint*," he snarled softly. "Learn your lesson for coming here on such a reckless impulse and placing yourself in the power of men whom you know nothing about."

"You're a cruel devil!" she flung at him, and when she tried to twist away from the wrapping of his whip he deliberately tightened it so she cried out.

"Feel my whip, and remember my words," he said, and he spun her free of the plaited leather, and as he turned away from her a flick of his hand brought Mehmed from among the palm and pepper trees of the great stone courtyard.

They spoke together and then he strode off and Sarah watched the billowing of his cloak against the sun-soaked wall of an arcade of tall columns – almost a cloister where he was abruptly lost among the dense shadows that contrasted with the golden sunlight.

"You will come, *sitt*." Mehmed spoke in his broken English, and she saw that he carried her suitcase and that, at least, was something of her own in a world of strangeness and a certain terror. She followed Mehmed into the *kasbah* through a great wooden door leading to a stairway that seemed to wind round and round itself. She felt like a prisoner being led to a tower, and so it turned out when they entered the room at the head of the stairs. It was completely circular, and lit by narrow, wood-meshed windows, as finely, intricately carved as lacework.

Sarah glanced around her, torn between fascination and those tiny waves of fear that swept over her every time she thought of the things which that blue-eyed devil had said to her. If he had meant to unnerve her, then he had succeeded! Almost unaware, she was clasping her hands tightly together as she looked around this room, high up in the stone *kasbah* of a man she had yet to meet . . . a man whose power was absolute in this part of the world.

Mehmed placed her suitcase beside the wide ottoman bed, and then with a salaam he withdrew and closed the high oval-shaped door behind him. She tensed, as if she waited to hear a key turn in the lock but there was only silence as the Berber walked silently away from her door. Of course, there was no need to lock her in. The *kasbah* was in the very heart of this desert province and if she ran out of here she could only lose herself in the strange

95

narrow streets where the houses crowded together as if sketched in charcoal by an artist who saw slantwise. *Souks* shadowed by latticework frayed and patched, and walls sun-scaled and old leaning verandas beneath flat rooftops. Shadows, menace, and the drip of water from wall-fountains. Men who walked robed, and women who went veiled ... Sarah saw it all in her imagination, and knew that come what may she must stay here and await what lay in store for her.

She gave a tiny uncontrollable shiver and felt very alone, and then she fiercely told herself that she mustn't give way to her nerves, and the best remedy for control was to concentrate on her present surroundings.

It was by no means a small room, panelled with a silvery wood that she supposed was cedar, and with a ceiling encrusted with gold flowers. Above the ottoman hung a fine mesh of netting, probably to keep out sand-flies and other tropical insects that might prowl in the night. Overhead hung lanterns of blue glass, blending with the fretwork of the windows to create a very oriental atmos-phere, especially as the window frames were surrounded by powder-blue tiles with raised designs. Like pale smoke over these tiles were curtains with a design of flowers, vines and trees showing through. Underfoot were rugs of tawny-gold with blue tracings in the rich wool, and against the walls was a matching armoire and toilet-table with an inlay of tortoiseshell. Here and there beside low ebony tables were big leather floor cushions, intricately embroidered with fine strips of leather in scarlet, gold and blue.

The toe of her shoe stirred the patterns of the rug on which she stood, of a thickness that made her want to kneel down like a lost child in this strangely beautiful room.

She knew that a *kasbah* meant a fortified palace whose rambling walls reached out to enclose the town, and those walls were pierced by battlements where the Khalifa's guard would stroll in their flowing robes. It was another world, still feudal, and ruled by a man whose personality had to match his courage and his charisma.

"I really am here," she told herself, staring across the circular room into a mirror with an arabesqued frame of wrought-iron. That was her red hair, and her eyes ... oh lord, how scared and big they looked, so that it was already difficult to think of herself as the soignée model who had posed in custom-made gowns.

She felt dry and her gaze dwelt on one of the low tables. On a brass tray stood a glass container of a rose-coloured liquid, and also a slim glass in a brass holder. There was also a dish with a transparent cover, making the ripe figs and dates look almost unbearably inviting. Oh, she had to take a drink of whatever it was in that carafe ... she had to accept this place or go quietly crazy.

Without further hesitation Sarah knelt by the table and poured about half a glass of the liquid and tentatively sipped it. Her eyes closed involuntarily, for it was delicious. Squeezed passion-fruit juice, she decided, with a dash of honey and lemon. Mmmm, she topped up her glass and drank it down like a thirsty infant. How good it tasted, making things seem a little less alarming. She took the lid off the fruit dish and bit into one of the ripe, almost purple coloured figs. It was like a blend of nuts and honey, and once again her eyes stole round this room with its disturbing blend of subtle fabrics, soft scents and splashes of barbaric colour.

Did it make her think of a harem, or was she letting her imagination run away with her? Her eyes dwelt on the soft luxury of the ottoman, on the floor cushions, and the various wall-hangings encrusted with gold and silver embroidery. She stared at an inlaid chest between two of these hangings, painted and bearing the same silvered arabesques.

Curiosity gripped her and she went over to the chest and lifted back the lid . . . at once she breathed an evocative scent and saw that it was stored with things of sheerest silk and the lightest imaginable velvet. Sarah was too well trained in the recognition of fine fabrics not to see at once that these garments were exquisite . . . and utterly Eastern. She lifted out a tunic that was a mere ripple of apricot silk over her fingers, hardly weighing more than a few ounces. She stroked a waistcoat of lime-coloured velvet, soft as a cat's fur.

This was a marriage chest, and these were bridal clothes . . . it was strange that she knew, and stranger still that she was so certain. Her fingers slid beneath the diaphanous legs of pearl-pale *serwals,* and touched the *broderie arabe* on the collar and cuffs of a kaftan in lovely peacock brocade. She lifted out a robe of apple-green, each hanging sleeve rich with silver embroidery.

Clothes fit for a princess . . . but why were they here in this room? Had the chest been left here and forgotten, for there was no telling how long these lovely things had been stored away. The garments of the East were curiously ageless, worn not only for their effect but for their coolness in a climate that was incredibly hot during the daytime. Sarah had already learned for herself how stuffy and un-comfortable a woman could feel in the desert in a pair of slacks that clung to the limbs. These floating tunics and trousers would be ideal, and no doubt the waistcoats were for evening wear, when the sun dropped and the air grew cooler.

Why were they here? Was she expected to wear them?

She led the lid fall and she backed away from the painted chest. No matter how inviting the thought was, she was an English girl who had to cling to her own identity and not give way to those insidious doubts and fears about what was to become of her now she was at Beni Zain. Why, why, why had she let out to the Khalifa's arrogant *aide-de-camp* that she hadn't told a soul she was coming to this outlandish place?

Then she gave a little cry as she almost tripped over one of the floor cushions, and as she was reminded again that she had this weak and troublesome ankle she sat down on the cushion and gritted her teeth in order to hold back the self-pitying, rather frightened tears. It was her own fault that she was here: impulse had driven her as far as Casablanca and it was only from there that she had actually been forced – yes, forced into coming to this barbaric, hidden city in the sandstone hills of Barbary.

The only consolation was that the walls of this room seemed so thick that they kept out the heat of the sun, and the *mesharabiya* work of the window screens maintained that coolness, being open to the elements through those intricate and delicate carvings.

Sarah had no idea of the time, for her tiny jewelled watch had stopped in the desert. With a weary little sigh she slid to the carpet and rested her head against the soft leather of the cushion. She yawned and vaguely wondered what else had been in that passion-fruit juice beside lemon and honey, for she suddenly felt very drowsy and her eyes were so heavy that they refused to stay open. No, she mustn't sleep . . . and the very next moment it seemed hardly to matter. *Mektub*. The hands of fate. Well, she placed herself in those hands, and all she could do right now was submit to her drowsiness and snatch a few minutes' sleep. It would help clear her head and brighten up her wits when the moment came for her to meet the Khalifa.

Her head drooped and she slid a little lower on the thick wool of the carpet . . . sleep enclosed her like that great cloak from a pair of wide shoulders, and for Sarah there was no more aching anxiety until she awoke abruptly to find the oil-lamps alight and flickering on the silvery patterns of the *damassin* wall hangings. She blinked, gave a little groan, and pushed the tumbled hair out of her eyes.

She carefully stretched her left leg and found herself on the ottoman instead of the floor, and there was a silk pillow under her head instead of the edge of the floor cushion.

She sat up and felt the hammering of her heart as she took a swift look around her . . . she didn't know what she expected to see, perhaps a tall figure with intense blue eyes, watching her as she slept, waiting for her to awake so he could inform her that she was, indeed, to be a companion . . . his.

But the circular room was empty but for herself . . . right now she was alone, but while she slept someone had entered and lifted her from the carpet to the bed. Her fingers gripped the filmy sheets and her nostrils tensed to the scent of cinnamon which seemed to be coming from the lamps. So it was night time, and she was quite certain now that there had been something in that delicious, rose-coloured drink which had made her sleep like a child, dreamlessly and unaware of being moved from the floor to the wide ottoman.

Hours had slipped away and the darkness beyond the windows seemed to intensify her feeling of being in another world. It increased her fears to the verge of panic, and suddenly she was scrambling off the bed and searching for the shoes which someone had removed from her feet. She found them and hastily put them on, then she made for the door and wrenched it open.

A lamp was alight outside, in a wall sconce that threw bars of shadow down those winding steps that led to that great courtyard. Clenching the handrail, Sarah made her way down the steps, feeling her head spin a little as they went round and round in a spiral, all the way to the ground. There she stood a moment, seeing ahead of her a stone archway that led out into the courtyard. It wasn't that she had any mad idea of running away, but she had to see someone, anyone, and demand to know what was to become of her.

As she made for the archway she became aware of a flickering red glow and she heard the sound of guttural voices, sounding excited and barbaric to her English ears. She stepped beyond the arching stone and caught her breath in amazement . . . a great fire was lit at the centre of the immense quadrangle and a group of robed men were standing around a great mat on which two other men were wrestling. Both were tall, their torsoes agleam in the flare of the fire, naked to the waist, with hard brown feet gripping the gound as they fought each other.

Sarah stared through a gap in the ring of spectators, and the barbarism of the scene made her more than ever certain that she had left civilization behind her for the rest of her days.

Then someone threw some more wood on the fire and as the flames leapt into the air, the face of one of the wrestlers was revealed like a bronze mask, the white teeth bared and the eyes filled with a devilish flame that was sheer blue instead of red.

"I might have known!" Sarah whispered the words to herself, and even as she did so those powerful brown arms suddenly lifted their opponent into the air and threw him bodily to the wrestling mat. As he lay stunned, a foot was planted on his chest, and there were shouts from the group of Berbers, and Sarah caught a name:

"El Zain, *baraka, baraka*!"

It was impossible, incredible, but true, for with a throaty laugh the winner of the bout threw back his head and acknowledged the name, then he caught hold of the great cloak that was tossed to him and threw it around his shoulders. He came striding from the group, the cloak like a dark wing around his glistening brown body, and he was coming straight towards Sarah, who like someone in a trance, or a nightmare, couldn't move a limb in order to escape from him. She could only stand there and feel the power and the strangeness of the man bearing down on her; she could only remember the things she had said to him in the desert, the names she had called the Khalifa of Beni Zain!

"So you couldn't stay away, *bint*. You had to come looking for me!" He stood over her, haughty, sure of his position, a kind of gold amulet glistening against his naked chest. "You slept well, I presume?"

"There was something in that drink, wasn't there?" She gazed at him with angry yet uncertain eyes. There was no longer a shadow of doubt in her mind that he was Zain Hassan bin Hamid, high lord of this place, who had let her make to him some of the most indiscreet remarks of her life. She felt as if she hated him all the more.

"You evidently enjoy playing games, El Zain, whether it's with a woman, or for the benefit of your tribesmen."

"I like to tease and I like to wrestle," he admitted. "I need my recreations like everyone else, and riddles are something of particular interest to the Eastern mind, and be assured I am of the East in every bone of my body. We invented the convolution of design, the everlasting detail that is as endless as the desert itself."

He reached up a hand to touch the vaulted arch in the shape of a horseshoe, with an arabesque of patterns deeply incised in the stone; wheels and suns, moons and crescents, with the name of Allah engraved among them.

As he ran his fingers over the stone, Sarah saw and breathed the savage gold of his skin, still marked here and there by the grip of his opponent's hands during that wrestling match. In the glow of the wall lanterns he was like some lithe and savage animal, and there rushed through Sarah's mind all that she had been told about the Khalifa — that he was strong enough to rule his people in his own way, and that once upon a time he had had a wife . . . and that soon after his birth his mother had been disposed of because this ruthless, blue-eyed creature had been thought to be the son of her lover.

Why had he not been killed at the same time . . . would the child have been disposed of had it been a girl?

"You are a riddle," she heard herself remark, a moment before she had to remember that whatever he was, above all he was high lord of Beni Zain.

"That makes two of us, *bint*, and what could be more intriguing than that a man and a woman should find each other a source of mystery. Come, I have to wash and change my clothing, and you will eat supper with me in my apartment –"

"But tell me," she broke in, "what are you going to do – am I to stay here or what?"

"Of course you stay." He said it decisively. "There is no question about that."

"Then I am to be the companion to your sisters – is that it?"

"Their companion has been selected. The widow of an Egyptian doctor, who is rather more intellectual than you, *bint*, who will expand the minds of those two."

"But what about me?" Sarah backed against the stone archway and felt as if her heart had come into her mouth.

"You?" His hand fell to her hair and she felt his fingers drifting from her temple to her earlobe. "You, my mercenary little *roumia*, I may decide to marry."

Sarah jumped as if she had been shot, and she was speechless as he led her into the *kasbah*, along a honeycomb of corridors and shadowy passages, into the very heart of his stronghold. Then that word he had used hit her again and she tried to pull free of his hand upon her elbow.

"I – I won't be played games with any more," she gasped. "Y-you can't do just as you like with people, and I happen to be English –"

"Yes, isn't that fortunate?" he drawled. "That is what I want, the English blood mixing with mine to produce a son of coolness, courage and stamina. And what an added bonus that you are a female I can fight with, who

103

won't be just a subservient object for me to caress."

"You're stark raving mad," Sarah flung at him. "You can't marry me against my will —"

"Here at Beni Zain I can do whatever I have a mind to do." And so saying he propelled her in through the door of what appeared to be a foyer, for it was quite bare of furniture and only a blue marble fountain played at the centre of it. There was another door beyond the fountain and Sarah struggled with him when they reached it. It led into his apartment and she wouldn't go in there with him, unless he dragged her by the hair.

"Ah, how you like to fight!" And suddenly his hands were gripping both her elbows and she was pulled close and breathlessly against his bare chest. His cloak fell to the floor and Sarah's eyes dilated as they filled with his bronzed face, so deeply clefted at the chin that it held a wedge of dark shadow. His eyes held hers, their glinting mockery almost beyond bearing.

"I hate you!" she choked. "You're a devil, but I'm not scared of you like everyone else — I'll find a roof and jump off it rather than end up in your arms!"

Powerful, tanned arms whose warmth she could feel right through the silk of her shirt. As she looked wildly up at him it was as if time had no meaning — as if eternity held its breath while she read his eyes and realised that her words, her intentions, her entire freedom, were as nothing to this man who had only to click his fingers and have his smallest whim served up on a silver plate.

"You — you can't mean to keep me here," she whispered.

"Have I not said it?" He spoke in what could only be described as a throaty purr, and the very next moment Sarah found herself in his private sanctum, and as he closed the door and shut them in together, she saw the bronze crescent set in the wood . . . that symbol of the East, stabbing her with all its implications. A woman, he had said, was an object of joy . . . a creature without a soul. He was of the East and he believed it . . . Sarah was of the West and she had to fight not to believe in a ruthlessness so absolute that he would disregard her pleas, subdue her struggles, and make her do exactly what he wanted.

"Why?" she asked. "Why me, El Zain?" She drew on her pride and faced him, but inwardly she was cold at the core of her and desperately aware of her own helplessness. She tried not to cringe as his eyes swept from her hair to her throat and down the entire length of her slim body.

"A man might think that you were fishing for a compliment," he drawled. "At this precise moment you look a trifle rumpled, but how the red hair flames about your white skin, and how the eyes blaze green as emeralds. Do I really have to put into words why I have a fancy to make you my *kadin*?"

"Even with this?" It was her only weapon, and she used it. "I have a stiff foot, El Zain. I walk with a limp. I'm maimed and not the perfect thing that the lord of Beni Zain might wish for."

"We have a saying in the East, *bint*. It is that nothing should be entirely perfect, for then the evil eye won't fall upon it. Under your feet are the magnificent carpets of Bokhara, but each one has a fault woven into it. Above your head are Moorish lamps, but in each one there is a piece of spoiled glass. Those *damassin* hangings look very gorgeous, but in the pattern there are certain gold and silver threads that have been deliberately twisted. We are a superstitious people, Miss Innocence, and I have good reason to believe in the evil eye."

"So have I!" she rejoined, and she looked directly into his face and let him know exactly what her thoughts were with regard to his eyes that a few moments ago had seemed to strip the clothes from her body.

He gave her an ironical bow as he accepted her accusation. "It makes not the slightest difference what you think of me, but were you quite wise to send the photograph that you did with your application to be a companion? It was despatched to me at Casablanca, and I sent back an immediate message to my emissary. Would you like to know what it contained? Yes, I am sure you are curious. 'Find out if she is a virgin', I ordered, and Kezam Zabayr, a man of wide experience, was able to report that he had actually spoken with this attractive creature and found her virtuous in body even if her mind was a little too occupied with pounds and pence."

"You – you damned devil!" Sarah glared at him and would have given her last breath to have got at those blue eyes and torn them out with her fingernails. "You and your cohorts, planning things so slyly – you won't get away with it! Some of my friends will realise that I'm missing and they'll make enquiries – "

"No doubt they will, in time," he agreed. "But by then, Miss Innocence, you will be the bride of Zain Hassan and there won't be a thing they can do about it, not a string they could pull that would release you from my custody. Unless, of course, they wanted a war on their hands."

"You're incredible," she gasped. "You really believe in your own self-opinionated power, don't you?"

"You had better believe it as well, *bint*. I don't waste my breath on empty threats, and the matter of our marriage is already in hand. Your dress will be sewn, your jewels selected, your body purified, your hands and feet hennaed, all within the next few days. You will also be well instructed in the words to be spoken at the ceremony; Arabic words that you will be made to learn. Do I make myself utterly clear?"

"I – I won't listen to you!" Suddenly like a frightened child Sarah flung her hands over her ears, but all the same she heard him laugh and the next moment he had taken hold of her, lifted her as if she weighed no more than a child and dropped her among the cushions of an enormous black and silver divan.

"Now if you've a mind to faint you may do it in comfort," he mocked. "Yes, you show unmistakable signs of being a virgin, and the strawberry is sweet, warm, plucked straight from its bed – and I won't have a child from a woman who has been used by any other man!"

Sarah stared at him through a wing of her red hair and the temptation was too great to resist. "I really fooled your emissary, didn't I?" she said swiftly. "Did he really believe me when I said I wasn't a woman of experience – of course I've had a lover. Do you really imagine that I didn't go to bed with my English gentleman?"

She watched his face through her tumbled hair, hardly daring to breathe as she took in that ferocious jawbone, the imperial line of the nose commanding the bold mouth and chin. Her heart thudded in her breast . . . he was strangely like a portrait she had once seen in a Bond Street gallery, of a certain wayward British soldier who had been painted in Arab robes.

She caught her breath as he suddenly leaned over her and caught hold of her hair, winding it around his fist and forcing her to look right up at him.

"The weapons of women are always devious ones, when they aren't putting poison in the cup, or a knife in the back. I could prove right now, *bint*, that you are as untried as my own sisters, a pair of girls who have been kept sheltered all their lives – "

"I've never been sheltered," she panted. "I grew up in a poor part of London, and I've always worked and made my own way – y-you know about models, surely? Men always run after them and tempt them with gifts and money. You said yourself that I have a mercenary streak in me – "

"You, *bint*, are leading yourself into a maze of desperate lies – come, *hilwa*, shall I take you right now and prove what is true or false about you? Shall I?" As he spoke he placed one knee upon the side of the divan, and the sensuous light of the copper and glass lamps shone down on the tawny skin of his shoulders and Sarah saw the flagrant male power in them . . . she shrank away as he leaned over her, the gold amulet swinging on its chain about his strong column of a neck. No man she had ever known had borne any resemblance to this one . . . never in her life before had she been so aware of absolute male authority combined with a savage, sensual enjoyment of her physical and mental terror.

"Brave words in a craven body," he mocked. "As if any woman of experience ever had that look in her eyes – she would know, you little fool, that she could use her charms even on me. I am but a man, eh?"

"You're a barbarian –" Her lips shook and she despised this terror that made her want to curl into a ball and bury her face deep in the cushions. Nothing and no one had ever made a coward of her before, but he had succeeded very thoroughly. Not even her accident and the pain of it had reduced her to this quivering heap of white skin, and knocking knees!

"Fool of a girl." His hand cupped her chin and his lean hard fingers pressed against the fine bones of her face. "I might well have carried out that threat, you know, then you would have been dishonoured, would you not? At least in marriage you will still have your virtue even if I take your chastity – you see, you blush!" He laughed in that low-throated way of his, showing the white bar of his teeth. "You blush to feel my hand, to see my bare skin, here where we are alone in my Eastern apartment, where on a European beach these things would be as nothing. The desert is different, *bint*. Here there is an intensity in all things, a deeper meaning to the giving and the taking. When we pray we mean every word. When we fight we are unafraid to die. When we make love it might last a night or an eternity. When we are dishonoured we have no more to live for."

"Kezam Zabayr said you were a widower," Sarah

crouched there among the cushions and she felt the tips of his fingers stroking down against her throat, so that somehow, anyhow, she had to make him stop touching her. "What happened – did she take a lover and had to be choked for it?"

Silence . . . that petrified stillness just moments before the leopard leaps at the throat of its prey.

Fingers closed on Sarah's throat, on the pulses that hammered under her soft skin . . . she gave a little moan as she was borne backwards until her neck was stretched painfully across the cushions.

"I would kill anyone else for saying that," he snarled. "But you I have a use for and I won't waste a long, hot trip across the desert in order to bring you here. I had a wife – Farah she was called, my joy! She was seventeen when the elders gave their approval of our marriage, and she was more lovely than you could ever imagine, slender, the colour of pale honey, with a deep bewitchment to her amber eyes. Real joy, they say, is not for any man on this imperfect earth, and I had Farah for only a few years. She died when our son was born, and it was her wish to be buried in the deep heart of the desert, and when at times I ride a horse to exhaustion, or wrestle with a companion, or take someone like you, I do it from the need of her that comes over me, to hear again her voice, her laughter, my name on her lips."

His fingers slackened from Sarah's throat, and he stood up to his full height, proud and hard, his thoughts lost in the past. "To marry again a Berber girl would remind me too painfully of what I lost when Farah closed her amber eyes and never opened them to me again. That was twelve years ago – a lifetime."

Sarah sat up, a hand at her throat, her green eyes fixed upon his bronze mask of a face. "If you have a son –"

"I had a son, *bint*. He was four and he looked like her – he was playing in the sands when a scorpion bit him. The venom went straight into a vein and there was nothing our doctors could do for that little boy – he died in agony in my arms, and how do I forget his pain and his fever, and her eyes in his small face, begging me to take away the hurt? As a prince of the Beni Zain he is buried here in the grounds of the *kasbah*, though it would have been my wish to have them together, the two people I loved, will always love, beyond you, *roumia*, with your white skin and your eyes like leaves of jade. You I will have, and from you another son for the Beni Zain. Is it understood?"

Sarah could only gaze at him in stunned bewilderment, but not for a single moment did she doubt the incredible truth of his story. Long ago he had buried his heart with a girl called Farah, and now he felt the time had come to marry again just for the getting of another son; a male child for his tribe, but one he would never love as he had that four-year-old who had died while playing in the sand.

This was strictly a matter of policy, and she was conveniently at hand with her slim, untried body, her undoubted Englishness, and the indisputable fact that an unkind fate had cut her free from the ties of her career.

He meant every word that he said . . . it was there in his face, so brown and hard and deeply clawed by sun-lines. It was there in his eyes that were as burning blue as the skies over the desert where his young wife was buried.

"*No!*" She felt that she cried out the word, but she only whispered it. "No – please!" She pressed her hands over her face, as if to shield herself from the implacability of his tawny features.

"Why not?" His voice was as hard and unrelenting as his face. "You say that you can no longer do the work for which you have trained, and I can give you comfort and a position even higher in life than could your Englishman. Wasn't that why you would have married him, to be a woman of means and position? Make no mistake that I am supreme chief of the Beni Zain and the woman I take for a wife has at her beck and call a large staff of servants, her own bodyguards so that she may, if she wishes, have the freedom of the desert to ride in. She may even come and go in the *medina* and have female friends of her own. Up to a point, Zahra, your life would be your own."

Zahra! With shocked green eyes Sarah studied this man who arrogantly supposed that she would fall in with his incredible wishes.

"No!" This time she did cry the word. "I wouldn't be your wife if you were the last man on earth!"

"Why?" His eyes glittered with an unholy blue light. "Because I am a Berber – a man of different skin and faith – a barbarian?"

"Because," she said distinctly, "I don't happen to love you!"

"Nor do I love you, *bint*," he said, with equal distinctness. "What has that to do with a business arrangement? A merging of two people with something to gain from the transaction? I provide you with the things most dear to your heart – clothes, jewels, comfortable surroundings – and you in return provide me with a boy child. I will tell you something, when you see blue eyes in the face of a desert man it means that he has Crusader blood in his veins. I fancy to have a son of your race, and let us say that you have fallen into my hands like a ripening fruit from a golden date palm."

In his hands! Those three words said it all for Sarah, and in a sudden attack of fright and panic she scrambled off the divan and attempted to make a dart for the door. She forgot her tedious ankle and its tendency to let her down at a crucial moment. Her foot bent sideways, pain shot into her leg, and she fell as if broken to the carpet, at the feet of this man who seemed to straddle her frightened body.

"Don't make me," she pleaded. "I'll wish you in hell

if you make me marry you – I can't, don't you see that? I – I have no feeling for you, and to have your child –"

"Yes, to have my child," he said deliberately, "you would have to lie in my arms and know me as you have not yet known any man."

"You're pitiless," she gasped. "You have no heart!"

"I quite agree, *bint*. My heart lies somewhere in the desert, and my pity was buried with my small son from the sweet, honey body of Farah. But you have beauty, and I am for the rest entirely a man."

"A man of iron, that's what you are!" Sarah caught at her lip, for her ankle hurt and her entire body was aware of a very new sort of fear, never felt in all the six years she had worked as a model – but then, in all those years she had never come up against a man like this one. "If I were to cry, you'd only deride my tears, wouldn't you?"

"I can't deny it," he drawled.

"If I were to scream, you'd slap my face to stop me."

"Perhaps not your face, but I would treat hysteria as it deserves to be treated."

"Marriage isn't the word for what you want – it's libertinage!"

"A good, sound English word, but if I meant to take liberties I wouldn't propose marriage. You are illogical, woman." He bent down and pulled her to her feet, but when her teeth bit down harder on her lips and a sudden drop of blood appeared, he suddenly swept her up in his arms and held her against his hard bare shoulder. "For my own part I find the prospect of making a child with you not at all disagreeable. I may even teach you, *bint*, to find a certain pleasure in being my *kadin*."

"I – I'd sooner be chewed up in the teeth of a tiger!" The fear, the temper, the infuriating awareness that she was powerless to fight against his demands, drove Sarah to a retaliation that in a saner moment she would have found

112

shocking. There below her eyes, within reach of her fingernails was that smooth tawny shoulder and with the blazing wish to hurt him overriding everything else she drove her nails into his skin and raked them down into his flesh as hard as she could. The blood sprang red against the dark gold torso and the scratches were sharp and jagged and painful-looking.

"You little *shaitana*," he snarled softly. "Now do you feel better?"

"Heaps!" she flung in his face. "I wish I had a knife – I promise you that would be in your back right now!"

His blue eyes warred with her blazing green ones. "Yes, *inshallah*, that will be quite a boy that you and I will have from this marriage – ah yes, you may scratch, bite and claw for all you are worth, Zahra, but it's written that you and I should come together at the full of the moon, when the elders of the Beni Zain are witness to our bridal. You will look quite gorgeous in your Berber wedding garments, with pearls in your flame-coloured hair, with the henna patterning those vicious little hands of yours, and nothing between us but the fire of your hate and the duty I have to give my people the next Hassan bin Hamid. It may well be a duty that I shall enjoy, Zahra."

"Don't – don't you dare call me by that damned Berber version of my name," she choked. "I won't stand for it!"

"No, you will lie in my arms for it," he mocked. "Zahra – flame flower, white ivory – white slave." He laughed at the anger and tears glittering together in her eyes, and through her tears she saw that his face had a look of pagan pleasure in her helplessness.

"I'll run off into the desert – I'll get away from you somehow," she said, and a tear broke and ran down her cheek to her anguished mouth.

"From this moment, *bint*, until you are very definitely mine, you will have a guard at your door. There is no getting away from me, for like my name I strike swiftly."

"Like a snake?" she asked, feeling the wetness on her face and hating herself for crying in front of him. "Is that what your name stands for? The snake in the garden who led me here with lies and false promises!"

"I can't recall that I lied to you, Miss Innocence."

"Oh God, yes, was I innocent! You pretended you were on the Khalifa's staff –"

"You presumed it, let me remind you. I was servant, chauffeur, *aide-de-camp* and procurer of his women, in that order, if I recollect the names correctly."

"And all the time you were laughing up your sleeve at me!"

"You asked for it, did you not?"

"It seems –" a sob caught in her throat, "it seems to me that I didn't ask to have my career blasted and to be taken in by a false advertisement –"

"Ah, but it wasn't false, *bint*. It was quite genuine, and it was your mistake to be so vain as to send to a stranger a photograph so striking that he couldn't resist meeting the original." Slowly, taking his time, he searched every bone, shadow and angle of her white face in its cloud of flamy hair. It was unbearable, the inquisition of his blue eyes, and Sarah turned her face away and found it buried against his warm shoulder. She shuddered . . . whichever way she turned he was there and there was no escape from him.

"Can't I appeal to your better self, if you have one?" she whispered. "Are you quite a devil in the shape of a man?"

"I am Zain Hassan bin Hamid, the sword of my people. I have to consider their future before my own inclinations, and the time has come when I must marry again – and surely the time has come when you should marry and let your beautiful body enjoy its natural functions. The camels, the sand-cats and the flying foxes all manage it quite

114

naturally, so why not a little tigress like you? Why be afraid?"

"If you have to ask that, El Zain, then you must be terribly insensitive." She made herself look at him and her eyes were shadowed by that fear . . . she hadn't known until now that she could feel so actively afraid of what he referred to as natural. "Have you no feelings at all – do you really imagine that I could *enjoy* giving myself to you?"

"What does it matter?" Quite carelessly he dropped her to the divan. "You are a woman, and you have a certain beauty – it will suffice. You will find the rewards to your satisfaction even if you find your husband not much to your liking. I go to take my bath, and I warn you that it will do no good to leave this room the moment my back is turned. Two members of my bodyguard are now on duty in the foyer, and I regret to inform you that they won't allow you to leave."

He left her, disappearing through an archway covered by a thick silk hanging. Sarah stared at it and the gold threadwork seemed to quiver with a life of its own.

This moment couldn't be real . . . but it was. He had to be playing a game with her . . . but she knew he wasn't.

She took hold of a cushion and ground her fingers into it . . . she wished she had hold of his throat and had the strength to strangle all those frightening things he had said to her. Oh God, how could she possibly marry a stranger? You had to be in love before you took that step, and all she felt for Zain Hassan bin Hamid was a wild sort of terror of his strength and his strange blue eyes in that face that was utterly of the desert.

He had no heart . . . another woman of his own desert heritage had taken the better part of him to her lonely resting place among the sand dunes and the hot golden sun. There she lay alone, parted from the man who would marry Sarah in order to provide the next heir to the leadership of the Beni Zain. His duty, he called it, to take for his wife a woman for whom he hadn't a fragment of feeling.

And she, Sarah Innocence, was that woman!

It was unbelievable . . . and yet she knew that she had to believe it. Curse him, and her own stupidity in accepting that flight ticket which had brought her to an impasse from which there seemed no way out.

CHAPTER SIX

HE was like a figure in parchment who had stepped straight
out of the tales of the Arabian Nights. It was he who
tutored her in the Arabic words she must learn for the
wedding ceremony, a venerable old man called Sheikh
Moulay who gradually taught her some of the rudiments
of a strange and difficult language. The words seemed to
tickle her throat when she finally managed to repeat them.

"What do they mean in my language?" she asked, for the
sheikh spoke English, but of a kind that reminded Sarah
of a dignified Victorian.

Sheikh Moulay caught at his beard and regarded her
with a deep twinkle far down in his wise old eyes. "They
say, my daughter, that you must be humble and obedient
to the wishes of your husband. That you will be faithful
in all ways, and be his comfort and solace at his command.
That you will look not at any other man and cast your
gaze upon the ground when another man should walk
your way. That you will be a good mother and rear your
children in the lore of the Koran, may it be blessed."

"But, Sheikh Moulay, I'm not a Moslem," she objected.

"It matters not, *sitt*." He rested his long-fingered, veined
old hands on an exquisite copy of the Koran, printed on
gazelle skin and bound in the most supple of Moroccan
leather. "That you are chosen of the Khalifa is all that
matters."

"Lord high and mighty!" she exclaimed, uncaring of
what she called him, and also instinctively aware that
Sheikh Moulay was too aged and wise in the ways of men
and women to take much notice of her outcries. She was
young, nubile, and the Khalifa wanted her. That was
enough for his people – at last he wanted to marry again

and they welcomed the event. There was nothing to be gained, and Sarah knew it with a clutch of fear at her heart, to beg of even this kind old man: "Please, don't let him do this to me!"

"There is honour in such a marriage for any woman," he said. "You must surely realise that? The daughters of some of our most prominent *caids* have grown up in the eager hope of being chosen by Zain Hassan to be the wife of his body and the mother of his sons."

His wife . . . his sons . . . with not a spark of *tendresse* to alleviate the terror that ran like ice water down Sarah's spine each time she thought of what lay ahead of her. "He said he couldn't marry another Berber girl because of being reminded of his first wife – did you know her, Sheikh Moulay? Was she very lovely – very much loved?"

"*Ay*, lovely as a desert dawn, sweet as wild honey, gracious of heart. We have a saying, *sitt*, that perfection is its own worst enemy because Shaitan cannot endure it and sets his eye of evil upon it. *Ay*, Farah was much loved by the young Khalifa, but now he is a mature man and he realises that paradise is beyond the stars and that here on earth we must expect the bitter with the sweet."

"I'm sure you realise, Sheikh Moulay, that he's forcing me into this marriage." That description of Farah had pricked at Sarah's pride . . . no one, certainly not the bridegroom, expected honey and joy from his second wife. In no way was she expected to measure up to the gazelle-like loveliness of that first bride of Zain Hassan, who didn't care a snap of the fingers that for Sarah this marriage would be loveless. All he wanted of her, his mercenary *roumia* as he had called her, was her body that could make sons for him . . . big, blue-eyed sons for the Beni Zain.

As it all swept over her, the images, the loveless possession, the memories she could never share with that intimate stranger, Sarah gripped her hands together until her fingernails broke the skin of her palms.

"The elders of the Beni Zain can't really wish him to marry a foreigner," she said. "I know nothing of his ways – they're all hopelessly strange to me."

"It is not for any of us to question the desires of the Khalifa." The old sheikh spoke rather sternly. "He knows his own mind, and a woman is but a woman."

"A creature without a soul," she said bitterly. "A prisoner with a guard at my bedroom door, and spies who watch me when I take a walk!"

"Only because you might foolishly wander off and be lost in the desert – out there you could die in the burning sun, or be picked up by nomads who might treat you in a bad way. You comprehend my meaning, *sitt*?"

"Oh yes." She gave a shudder. "The desert is not exactly a garden of Eden for a woman, is it, one way or the other? The nomadic woman trudges from one well to another and gives birth to her children on the sands. The bride of a Khalifa is kept in seclusion and must be obedient to all his arrogant demands – I don't love the man, you know! I find him overbearing and utterly ruthless. Tell me, what would your people do if I took a fit into my head to knife him – he might act like some god, but he's only made of flesh and blood, and I don't imagine that his bodyguard actually share his bedroom of a night."

Sheikh Moulay gazed at her with eyes that were suddenly as hard as stone. "Hurt one hair of his head, *sitt*, and you will have the life and breath choked out of you."

"I thought that punishment was reserved for unfaithful wives," she rejoined. "If I put a knife into his precious heart I thought at least that I'd be torn asunder by wild horses."

"You might indeed," the sheikh said, quite seriously. "Zain Hassan has proved to be a strong leader, often a very understanding one to the Beni Zain, and a mere woman who harmed him would learn about hell before she died.

In some ways time has stood still here in the desert, and who would hear your screams across those many miles of silent sands?"

No one, she thought. There really wasn't a soul to care what became of her, for she had lived in a world where success was everything, and popularity a bright little globe that could fizzle out as quickly as it lit up.

A few people might ask casually what had become of Sarah Innocence, that slim young thing with the lovely walk, and someone might reply that she had probably gone off to Scotland where she had cousins; or had maybe got quietly married and settled for suburbia.

No one, not a soul, would ever dream that she was in some far region of Morocco, being tutored in the Arabic responses to a Berber bridegroom . . . a captive in his castle, watched night and day, and more desperately scared as each day passed and drew her closer to that moment when the high wooden door of the bridal chamber was closed for the night and she found herself in the arms of El Zain.

"Did you know his mother?" Sarah suddenly asked the old sheikh.

"Yes, but she is not spoken of, by him or anyone else. Come, repeat again the marriage vows and try to get the inflection as correct as you can –"

"Why mustn't she be mentioned?" Sarah persisted. "Was it such a sin, after all, when her child was reared to the leadership of the Beni Zain? Why he was allowed to live?"

"Because – and I really shouldn't tell you this – the man who fathered him was greatly loved by that foolish woman's husband, the Khalifa of those days. He was a great soldier, and I will say no more! Zain Hassan would be furious if he knew I had talked to you of the matter – now let us return to our lessons."

"You mean he's ashamed of what his mother did?"

"*Ay*, ashamed. He grew to regard the then Khalifa as his father, but he knew of the affair."

"Was the soldier a European?" Sarah had to ask; she had to know. "Tell me, please, and I promise never to repeat your confidence."

"You have looked into his eyes, *sitt*, so you can make your own guesses. But the name of this man is never mentioned, for he is too greatly revered for his courage to allow of any scandal to be attached to his memory. Suffice it that the foolish woman led him astray, as women will, and she paid the price. He was not, let me assure you, a man to look with lust at women, but this one time it happened and when the child was born, and it was a boy, there was no question of that precious life being put out like a candle. It carried the precious seed of great courage, stamina, leadership, and so it has been proved. El Zain is indeed a sword of a man."

"But the woman died," Sarah said, in a softly shocked voice. "Wasn't that abominably cruel – after all, she was his mother."

"She was unfaithful, and in those days there was little mercy – it was considered a crime."

"Is it still a crime?" Sarah asked. "What if I –?"

"I would advise you not to talk in such a way." It was the turn of the sheikh to look shocked. "That is shameless talk, *sitt*, and I close my ears to it. Now, to our lessons!"

"Just tell me one more thing and I promise not to ask another question – please." Sarah's green eyes pleaded with the sheikh. "This soldier, the real father of Zain Hassan, did he stand by and see this poor woman – did he? When he had made love to her and brought about her downfall –"

"By the time the child was born the father had died." The weathered old hands gripped the Koran. "I don't know, perhaps it was a kind of justice but a cruel one. He died in England, *sitt*, in a road accident, and now ask

121

me no more. It was all long ago and is partly forgotten, so let the dead lie in peace."

Sarah gave a sigh, for it was all a sad confusion, and could not be imagined as possible anywhere but here in the far desert, where passions might flame like the hot sun itself, and retribution be as chilling as the nights when the sun went down. So this man who had a fancy for a British bride was partly of that blood himself — somehow Sarah didn't doubt that the soldier had been British. She knew that many French soldiers had lived and fought in the desert, but those eyes, they were not Gallic but Celt . . . blue, intensely blue as a pair of sapphires, the elongation of their shape inherited from his Berber mother — poor thing, perhaps married to a cold man and pining for a little romance with that tall, mystic, blue-eyed warrior from another land.

"You have guessed, *sitt*?" Sheikh Moulay was staring at her across the ebony table where they worked on her Arabic.

"I think so." Sarah looked a little stunned. "It's incredible but true, isn't it?"

He inclined his head. "Never speak of it to the Khalifa. He loved deeply the man who reared him and he reverences his memory —"

"Even though that same man was responsible for his mother's awful death?"

"Even so, my daughter. Berbers are a mysterious and very ancient people, and here in the high hills of Beni Zain they keep to their old ways, stretching back to your Bible. The adultress, then, was stoned, and believe me to be choked is quicker, more humane."

"Humane!" Sarah shuddered. "And I must marry your Berber chief!"

"If it is the will of Allah, may his name be blessed."

"It's the will of Zain Hassan and you very well know it and are too loyal to him to say that it's wrong to make me submit to him." Sarah's eyes were the colour of dark jade, haunted and accusing, and shadowed by the lonely terror of a girl surrounded by people to whom the arranged marriage was all too familiar. The needs of the tribe came first, and love was little more than a romantic nonsense.

"If I were a Berber girl, Sheikh Moulay, it would be different. But I'm used to my freedom, of going my own way and being my own mistress. You're condoning a crime! You are!"

"Hush, my daughter, you are seeing djinns and wind devils where there are none. My lord Zain Hassan is no monster – he will be good to you in his own way, but a man must marry and the tribal leadership be secured for the future."

"Is he such a brilliant leader? He bears the name of the former Khalifa, but he's a –"

"You will refrain from that word, *sitt*." The old eyes flashed. "A man is a leader if he proves his powers. This one is a natural, daring, feared and respected head of the Beni Zain."

"Is he loved?" she asked. "That's problematical, isn't it? Fear and love don't go hand in hand."

"I wonder," the sheikh mused, and his eyes dwelt steadily on her rebellious face, the flamy hair secured in a snood as it must be when she was outside the *serayi* and ensconced with the frail old man in his alcove in the grand hall of the *kasbah*. He sat among cushions, and upon first meeting him Sarah had wondered how old he might be. He seemed acquainted with events which had happened long ago in the tribe and his fine old face was deeply seamed. She was allowed to be alone with him because he was a venerable teacher; if he had been a younger man none of this would be allowed, that she sit and talk in this vein to a Berber other than the one who was to be her husband. Sarah was learning the rules but she wasn't growing to like them. They made her furious at times, especially when she walked in the garden courts and was aware of the Khalifa's guards silently watching her.

"You are a woman," said Sheikh Moulay, "and compassion is the gift of women, so can't you have a little pity for a man who lost a boy-child of only four summers? Time does not truly heal, you know, it only stitches a skin over a wound that goes on aching."

"It was a tragedy," she said, "but are you sure it hasn't made him hard and unfeeling? It does that to some people – it closes up the heart."

"Would you have Zain Hassan open his heart to you, *sitt*?"

"No – yes, enough to let me go back to my own sort of life!"

"But whatever is written in the book of destiny is unalterable, *Nourmahal*."

"*Nourmahal?*" she repeated after him. "What does it mean?"

"Light of the harem. Will you not be that when the day of the wedding arrives? Desire is the gateway into the rose garden –"

"I – I don't want his desire – I want my freedom!" She gave the old sheikh an imploring look. "Can't you help me? I'm so unhappy!"

"You are a little afraid, and what woman isn't when she contemplates marriage and all that it means."

"Oh, but don't you see, Sheikh Moulay, it would be different if I loved him, but I feel only outrage that he should keep me here and arrange this marriage as if I'm just an *object*, without a will of my own. Wouldn't you help me to get away? Arrange a camel and *haudaj* for me, and a guide –?"

He shook his head. "It would be a madness, my daughter, for Zain Hassan has eyes in the back of his head, and my life would not be worth ten grains of sand if he discovered that I had sent you off in the desert in the uncertain hope of ever getting less than heat stroke. Be resigned to what he asks of you – you are beautiful, and it has always been written that one day you would belong to a man. In many ways Zain Hassan is an unusual man, and love, if it is that for which you pine, is a restless, changeable emotion, not to be relied upon. Give El Zain his sons and you will never want for anything, I promise you."

"Oh, I don't doubt that he'll lavish upon me all the silks, scents and jewels of Arabia," she said bitterly, "so long as I do my duty and become *enceinte* as soon as possible. What if I give him a daughter?"

"He will accept her and hope that next time you will have a son." The old sheikh smiled at her look of tragedy. "Women were born to the destiny of motherhood, and it has its compensations. Why go on tormenting yourself? You are far too young to thrash your brain with so many thoughts, for come what may life is to be lived, and I am told that life had become empty for you in your own country. It was surely loneliness that drove you here in the first place?"

"Yes, I was lonely, but I thought to be a companion –"

"You will be a companion, *sitt*, but to the brother instead of the sisters. It is bound to prove more exciting, is it not?"

"You're laughing at me, Sheikh Moulay," she accused. "You think I'm an awful fool because I make such a fuss about marrying your lordly barbarian chief. I'm a person, not just a body. I have my rights and he's striding rough-shod over them – and I hate him for it!"

"We have a saying that hate and love were twin stars that were struck asunder in a storm, and now they eternally seek to come together only to strike sparks off each other. Beware when you think you see hate, for you may be looking at love."

"You have a lot of sayings, Sheikh Moulay, that are very picturesque, but they're just stories without any reality to them. I know what I am, I'm just a prisoner here, and you and his sisters and all the others condone what he does because you're all afraid of him. He wears the blue cloak and the golden head-ropes, and he has that look about him that could make a tiger turn tail. I don't know what he was like when Farah was married to him, but I know how he affects me!"

Oh yes, how it could sweep over her, the recollection of his eyes upon her, the eyelids drooped lazily. "You will not wear the shirts and trousers," he had informed her. "The proper clothes have been provided and your *fatima* will dress you in those from now on . . . and I do beg of you not to tell me to go to hell either in words or in looks. If you refuse to be dressed by your *fatima*, then I shall come myself to your room and ensure that you are clad as a woman and not as a fake boy, albeit a rather charming one. I am not, *bint*, a lover of boys."

Lover . . . the word evoked images that she hardly dared to imagine. Sheikh Moulay, a kind and understanding man, had refused his help, and there was nothing she could do but learn these outlandish vows and try not to quake in her embroidered *babouches* each time she envisioned what those vows entailed.

Patiently, with kindness, the sheikh took her through the lesson once again, teaching her the throaty, almost menacing quality of his language. The fountains played beyond the shade of the archways, and the high-carried leaves of the palm trees were like etchings against the blue sky. Towards noon the heat began to rise, like a saffron cloak that pressed against the skin. Sarah rose to her feet, for the sheikh would turn eastwards and say his prayers, take coffee and a little food, and rest during the afternoon.

"I will see you in the morning, my daughter. Think on our conversation and take heart."

"I'll try, Sheikh Moulay." She stood there in her soft silk kaftan and slippers of pomegranate red with tip-tilted toes. She felt and looked delicately strange in the garments, but they were remarkably cool and comfortable, and she would never give that barbarian the satisfaction of robing her.

She gave a little bow and left the old man to his prayers, hearing as she went into the fountain court the Moslem prayer-call from the minaret tower of the *kasbah*. It was profoundly oriental, like everything else that surrounded her, and though the mèn faced east, their faces like bronze castings in the boldness of the sun, the women of the household went about their duties, for they had no right to ask or expect a paradise where there would be palm trees and pomegranates, fountains and fragrant gardens — and damsels with large eyes. That was the heaven reserved exclusively for the men, and it made Sarah smile as she wandered beneath the large shining magnolia leaves and breathed the heavy scent of Persian lilac.

She caught the whisper of the chennar trees, and when she glanced that way she saw the slight movement of a white robe, with tucked into the leather belt a curving knife. One of the guards who was always on the watch in case she took a fit into her head to slip away, but she wasn't quite a fool and knew that she could never make it across the desert without transport and a guide and adequate water and food for the journey.

From the walled roof of her room, with a pierced parapet all the way around it, she could see the desert and its vastness, the aspect of loneliness, and appalling daytime heat that filled her English heart with awe. She would never dare such a place on her own, for that would be sheer madness, but sometimes in the evening, just before she was escorted to the apartment of the Khalifa, she would stand on her rooftop and watch the huge stars mantling the gigantic sweep of some of the sand dunes. Men would sometimes ride in through the great walled gates of the *kasbah*, strangely lost in time on their long-legged camels, and she wondered would she have wanted to leave if she could have stayed in the capacity of companion to the two pretty half-sisters of the man who had chosen, instead, to court her as his prospective bride.

Sarah would press shaking fingers against the bones of her face, and feel the tremor in the curve of her lips. Her heart would beat with a frightened prayer when she thought of the hard bold lips of Zain Hassan on hers, taking, demanding, making her submit to him in a marriage that bore no relation to anything she had visualised with Peter Jameson. Life in the English country, in a gracious Tudor house, with dogs dashing in and out of the high-ceilinged rooms with their many mullioned windows. Walks in the woods and across the downs, friends from town for the weekend, and tea and toast before a great log fire in the afternoons.

The shattered dream of a poor girl who had worked hard to achieve the poise and finish which had attracted a young country gentleman . . . and now this, her red hair and her slim body that could wear gracefully any garment at all, even the timeless fashions of the East, to adorn the *serayi* of a man who was totally foreign to her despite what she had learned about his birth. That dash of European blood meant nothing; by upbringing and inclination he was a Berber to his bones. He thought and looked like one; he had the same tigerish grace of body, and on camel or horseback he was one with the animal.

He would make love like a Berber, with a savage passion that would hold a single burning purpose, to have from the union a male child to take the place of that other small heir to the Beni Zain . . . the son he had loved because Farah had borne him.

For her, Zahra as he called her, there would be no

tendresse, if that was what she hoped for. Perish the thought! She was good-looking enough to suit his purpose, and she was alone in the world, and she had no doubt that it was in his blood, his liking to take booty – and that was all she represented to him, a piece of booty that he could use to his advantage.

She wandered past an old water-wheel that splashed among the huge geraniums, the big blue poppies, and the overhanging clusters of pink oleanders. She breathed the essence of cypress and pepper, a mingling of sharp-sweet scents, and watched the butterflies that might have been shaped from coloured silk flying among the white and wine flower-bells of the jasmine that grew in great scented clouds wherever there was a wall to cling to.

She let her gaze rove beyond the towering bulk of the palms and the sun caught the wings of a hawk and it seemed to be made of gold.

There was no denying the beauty of the garden courts, and the craggy appeal of the *kasbah* itself, a place of twisting stone stairs and robed figures who salaamed when they saw her, or gave her a long stare of wonderment. There were corridors of filigreed archways, where chameleons with jewelled backs panted in the etchings of shadow. The place was medieval, a Berber lord's fortress with great wooden doors the double height of a man . . . whispers of Barbary pirates and Christian slaves followed Sarah on her explorations, walking in tune with the silent-footed guard who never intruded but was always there, sometimes the bearded Raschid, and at other times the incredibly handsome Daylis.

It was impossible not to be faintly amused at times, especially when she took a lunch-basket into one of the concealed *zaribas* and casually invited her guard to share a pastry of spiced meat and onion, or *shish-kebab* in a tasty roll of bread, followed by a luscious peach or a fresh fig.

It was because she wasn't supposed to do this that she took a wayward delight in doing it. Raschid was always very polite and formal and never took advantage of the invitation, but Daylis would flash his perfect teeth and accept from her hand a pastry or a roll. Neither he nor she understood a word of each other's conversation, but Sarah found it satisfying to disobey the Khalifa in any way possible, and Daylis was finer looking than any Valentino of the old silent screen and it had to be a boring occupation, having to follow her from place to place.

In and out of fascinating byways of uneven stone, with a grotto effect of blue-purple shadow, and down many, many steps to streets of mystery and tiny shops like holes in the thick walls, where the air was richly spiced and she saw dusky-eyed girls draped from head to toe like nuns, yet with a sensuous flow to their walk that denied the cool chastity of the woman whose body was her fortress. Their eyes were incredibly lovely, embedded in long lashes and applications of *kohl*, a tinkle of beads and bells from beneath those long skirts, from the anklets that added to the sensual charm of the way they walked.

Had Farah looked like these girls? Sarah longed to know. Taught from girlhood to be a pleasant source of wonder to a man?

One evening Sarah applied *kohl* to her eyes, having found the cosmetic in a little gold bottle in the painted chest in her room, and with it she wore a bead mask and a scarf of silk bought in the *souk* with the aid of Daylis.

Zain's blue eyes burned into her until she went hot all over, and then he laughed deep down in his throat. "You look as if you are off to a *bal masqué*," he drawled.

"It was at your insistence that I wear harem clothes," she retorted, flinging off the bead mask and the gauzy scarf. "I wanted you to see that I can never take on the semblance of one of your honey-skinned Berber girls. They walk beautifully, don't they?"

A wistful, lost look had come into her green eyes in their shading of *kohl*, that oriental cosmetic made from powdered wood-ashes, crushed mother-of-pearl slowly burned with a chameleon skin. Once upon a time she had moved with a grace which had made people turn their heads to watch her go by. Her way of moving had been her way to fame, and now she had this weak foot that was like a halter tying her to this man who insisted that she dress like a Berber girl so he could be amused at her expense.

"Were you trying to emulate the gazelle?" He bent to a cheroot box of hammered brass on one of the low tables and the copper lamps cast a jewelled shadow over his face, and over the brown skin of his throat, and the powerful arms where the sleeves of his tunic divided.

"I'm more of a jack-rabbit," she retorted, "I hop along." She turned away from him as he lit his cheroot and regarded her with eyes whose lids were lazily drooped in amusement. In the informal wear of tunic and male *serwal*, those trousers with tapering legs that hugged the calf, he was as disturbing as a large tawny cat that was relaxed without ever losing a shred of alertness. She felt that from an infant he must have grown up like that, as if at no time did he lose awareness that he carried in his veins, and in his eyes, a haunting reminder to his people that his mother had sought love from a foreigner outside the bounds of her husband's *serayi*. There had to be those of the tribe who didn't fully approve of a leader who wasn't fully entitled to be called Hassan bin Hamid. No doubt he had been legally adopted by the former Khalifa, but he struck her forcibly as a man who wouldn't easily forgive the transgression of a woman; his mother's behaviour had deprived him of some of his pride, and even his adoration of Farah had not softened his heart. Her untimely death had only hardened him.

Sarah saw it in his eyes, felt it each time she was alone

with him. He would look mockingly at her in these soft Eastern fabrics, and yet she was ever aware that if she wore her own Western clothes he would deliberately return her to her room and stand over her until she changed into one of the beautiful kaftans and the almost transparent *serwals* that the women wore.

She was being taught to obey him . . . and yet at the same time he took a subtle delight in saying things that aroused her temper so that all too often their suppers together culminated in a blazing argument. When that happened his eyes smouldered with a devilish pleasure in his bronzed face, and Sarah could have scratched them out for being so cruelly amused by her and the way he could set the spark to the tinder of her temper.

God, how he had the beautiful, cruel eyes of a devil!

Tonight they took supper in his private solarium, which opened right out to the milky glow of a crescent moon, reminding her of how the moon was growing until soon, all too soon it waxed full and she would not be escorted back to her own room after an evening with Zain Hassan.

As she gazed through the *mesharabiya* of the great balcony she could feel under the soft leather of her slippers the Jebel-Amour rugs, with their pattern of tigers and orchids in a setting of silvery-blue moons and stars. The solarium itself was sparsely furnished with gold-tawny floor cushions of huge proportions, coffee tables inlaid with beautiful woods, and a long divan in its own alcove. Far below her in the moon-shot darkness she could hear the plaintive barbarity of a desert song . . . was it a song of love . . . that splendour of the heart, that passionate attachment that made a wonder of all the world?

"Of what do you think, *gazella*?" In his silent way he had come across the carpets and she shivered involuntarily as his fingers slid across her shoulders, making a tiny sound of static against the shimmering green silk that she wore, like that of a dragonfly's wing.

"I'm thinking that if the desert wasn't so vast I'd run from you," and as she spoke she could feel the steely brilliance of his eyes upon her hair, drawn away from her brow into a shining conch-shell.

"I know it, *bint*. The moon grows bigger each night and the heart of the gazelle tells her that the hunter is closing in on her. The pretty, feckless gazelle who runs until she breaks her heart . . . don't do that, Zahra, for you wouldn't deprive me of the pleasure of your company, would you?"

"The pleasure of taunting me," she rejoined. "Of forever getting a kick out of how easy it was to entice me into your trap."

"Believe me, Zahra, you would not have enjoyed being a *dame de compagnie* to a pair of sweet but giggling girls. You were made to be the companion of a man and in your heart you know it. Such skin and eyes, and hidden fire, to be wasted on my little sisters. I have a great affection for both of them, but they will be much better with this lady from Egypt who will arrive here when she has settled her affairs in Cairo."

"Doesn't it worry you that I'd prefer to be with Lallou and Belkis? I like both of them, which is more than I can say for you. No doubt they had a nicer mother –"

Sarah hadn't meant to go that far, but he drove her to it with his taunts, and she tried not to flinch when his fingers dug into her upper arm and he swung her round to face him. If she had expected a sort of ashen anger, then she was disappointed. He merely looked at her with eyes as hard as stones.

"You have no courtesy as a fighter," he drawled, "you always like to hit below the belt. Don't wrestle with me, *bint*, for I know all the dirty tricks of the *savate* and I kick like a camel."

"You'd kick someone smaller than you, who happens to be lame?" As she tilted her nose at him, he took hold of her shining shell of hair and gave it a tug that drew her head backwards until her slim white neck was taut and the tendons hurt. "Unless I do something drastic with you, that cursed lameness will torment you to your grave! Tomorrow you will ride with me!"

"No!" Pain and panic welled into her green eyes. "Not that – you know I couldn't bear it! I never want to go near a horse ever again, a-and your damned horses are full stallions – I've heard them screaming at each other in your stables and the other day –"

"Yes, the other day two of them got at each other and you heard them fighting. This is a desert province, not a gentle country seat like Windsor or Amersham; here we don't castrate the stallion and rob him of all his spirit, which once taken away from him can never be passed on to the future breed of pure Arabian horses. You will ride again, for there is no enjoyment – short of one other – that is more pleasurable than a gallop in the dawn winds when the desert is cool before the start of the day. You will know that, I insist on it. Added to which I don't like fear in a woman, and your particular brand can be cured."

"It can't," she insisted, feeling inside her that spiral of rising panic when she thought of mounting a horse again and having that first pleasure in riding turned into a sudden nightmare when the animal cut loose and bolted and flung her headlong into a vortex of pain. "I won't be bullied by you into doing something that gives me the horrors, and gives you the pleasure of being cruel!"

"Don't be a child," he said crisply. "I can understand your fear, but it has to be overcome, and the only way is that you ride again. I often go on journeys to the outer areas of Beni Zain to visit those of our tribe who pasture the herds of camel, goat and sheep, and I should want you to come with me and it is more convenient if you ride your own horse without being led on camel-back. The other alternative would be for you to be kept very much in purdah any time I am away from the *kasbah* for any length of time – would you enjoy that?"

Shut up – guarded like some harem slave – watched night and day in case she followed his mother's example and took a lover!

Sarah gave him a defiant look, unaware that the addition of *kohl* made her green eyes look almost tragic. "You know how much I'd hate being a virtual prisoner here in your great stone castle, El Zain, and though you haven't a scrap of feeling for me as a person – only as an object – you have a niggling little worm in your mind which makes you wonder just what I'd do during your prolonged absences. The guards are very good-looking, aren't they, or do you plan to lock me up with eunuchs?"

He stared down at her and tiny points of fire were smouldering in his eyes. "I'd break your lovely neck and you know it," he said, so softly that it was like a rasping murmur in that strong brown throat.

"Perhaps I'd prefer that to being everlasting at your beck and call," she rejoined. "Your thing, your slave, to do your bidding and no one else's. Where you should have a heart you have a stone, which I don't doubt you carried away from Farah's grave in your heat-blasted, eternal, damned desert. The thought of riding there with you gives me no thrill – how do you plan to get me on horseback? Are you going to throw me across the saddle-bow like a sack of potatoes?"

"If necessary. One way or the other you will ride, for in every way I recognize that you are different from Farah – as unlike as a honey-spiked fruit is to a sharp green pepper. Purdah would indeed be a purgatory for you, would it not?"

She shivered at the bare thought, and then shivered again as she saw him leading her to one of his high and handsome Arabian stallions, taking hold of her and tossing her into the saddle. He would do it, and she had to choose long days, weeks, shut up in the *serayi*, or the quick brutal medicine of what he called the cure for her fear of riding.

"The remedy lies with you," he said in an unrelenting voice. "I offer you the freedom of the desert, or the captivity of the castle. Take your choice, Zahra."

"My name is Sarah," she said icily. "So now you are the *el hakim* who knows the cure for my complaint – what a clever man you are! No wonder the Beni Zain bow down to you!"

"You fiery little *bint*!" Suddenly his arms were bands of steel about her body and he was lifting her, carrying her to that deep divan with its hoard of cushions. He sank down with her and she was trapped by his firm, strong body, feeling the brush of his lips across the hollow of her throat.

"Don't do that –!" She twisted and turned in a fruitless effort to avoid his lips and evade his arms, but she might as well have been a fish on a hook, or a moth in a net. She had watched his abominable strength the other day, when unseen by him she had witnessed that stallion fight and the way he had flung between the pair of rearing, screaming horses and caught at their manes, twining into the horsehair the lean fingers he had twined into her red hair. He had snarled Arabic at the furious horses and somehow his dangerous position between the two had fired the stable hands with the courage to help him separate the stallions before they killed each other. They had been led back to their stalls, kicking and bucking and showing their teeth . . . and he had laughed . . . this tawny devil had stood there in the hot sunlight, his tunic plastered to his chest and shoulders, and he had put back his head and let forth a deep laugh of pure enjoyment in a danger which could have left him trampled and broken on the stones of the courtyard.

"You're inhuman," she panted. "You delight in

everything that's cruel and brutal –"

"You can say that, *rezel*, right now when you lie in my arms and my kisses are on your skin?" He lifted himself on an elbow and gazed down at her, taking in her every feature and paying deliberate attention to her shapely mouth. "That such lovely lips should be capable of uttering such unkind remarks about a man – are you frigid, I wonder, and have never murmured sweet nothings in a receptive ear?"

"Your ear will wait for ever," she rejoined. "Go to one of your Berber dancing girls if you wish to be told a lot of sweet lies."

"Do you think that women only pretend to like my company?" He quirked an eyebrow. "I could make you, even you, my *bint*, come to heel if I wished. Shall I demonstrate?"

"What do you mean?" She stared up into those chatoyant eyes with their changing hues from deep blue to the leaping flame at the heart of a fire . . . she felt the leap of apprehension that her heart gave as those little flames began to burn deep in his eyes.

"Must I use explicit language?" he drawled, and with deliberation he traced with his fingertips the curve of her cheekbones, moving them slowly to her temple and down again into the soft hollow behind her left ear. "A woman usually knows what a man means when he touches her, it is called the language of the senses, but I begin to think that you are going to need a lot of melting. It could be most diverting, especially for a man who has only to click his fingers when he wants divertissement."

Though his touch was featherlight on her throat, the meaning in his words went through Sarah like a shaft. She lay there beneath his hard body, crushed among the cushions, wanting with all her heart to fight him and yet unable to because she had suddenly lost all her strength. Her limbs felt boneless and she heard her own little moan

137

as he gathered a handful of her hair and pulled her face to his, to the warmth and hardness of his lips that took her mouth, her breath, and for endless moments made her live only through him.

Nothing else was real but the throbbing of nerves where his lips touched and his hands disturbed, tousling hair and silk and her deepest reserves.

"You see," very slowly he drew away from her and his lips ran down the sensitive skin of her inner arm, "it is possible for even you to enjoy the sensation of being kissed."

"I – I didn't enjoy it," she protested, "you forced that on me!"

"Like medicine, eh, to be taken with tightly closed eyes?" He stood up and left Sarah alone among the cushions, then for a second he bent over her and his eyes looked deeply into hers. "They call it the divine savagery of desire, my *bint*. It's a little less painful than having a tooth pulled."

Her skin burned beneath that look in his eyes . . . the look of a man who knew all there was to know about women and was in no doubt about her lack of experience. She had been a model among very modern people, but none of it had taught her how to deal with a man who didn't know the meaning of denial.

"Yes, it is you or chicken *cous-cous*," he drawled. "Sit up, Zahra, for my manservant comes with our supper and you look – by my eyes you look as if you have just learned the difference between men and women."

He stood to his full height and she sat up dazedly as there came a knock at the door and it opened to admit Mehmed with the large silver tray on which were various dishes of food under conical wicker lids. Sarah's nostrils tensed as in with Mehmed came the aroma of rich spiced food and the inimitable coffee brewed on an open fire, which made the tip of her tongue steal around her lips, still warm and rather bruised from that encounter with Zain Hassan's demanding mouth.

"Just here, Mehmed, if you please." He indicated a table near the divan, with its pattern of running gazelle inlaid in the satiny wood. The tray was lowered and settled on the table, and not once did the manservant glance at Sarah. She was the Khalifa's woman and not to be stared at in the presence of the lord . . . Sarah couldn't help but feel grateful for the courtesy, for she knew that her hair was tousled, her dress somewhat disarranged, and one of her slippers had tumbled off her foot. She felt quite sure that she looked manhandled!

Mehmed salaamed and left them. "*Cous-cous*?" drawled Zain Hassan, and very casually he sat down beside her and removed the lid from the largest dish on the silver tray.

CHAPTER SEVEN

"THAT is one invitation that I won't refuse," she said, still very nervous of him as he uncovered the dish of chicken baked golden on a bed of rice, with tiny sprouts, butter beans and carrots. It looked good and the aroma made her feel hungry despite the physical shaking up she had received at his hands.

He handed her a slice of bread and she had to move nearer to the table and consequently nearer to him in order to feed herself. Eating with her fingers was becoming a habit and she was getting quite good at it, but she couldn't yet roll a ball of semolina and toss it with expert ease into her mouth – as he could.

Even as she ate her delicious supper Sarah still felt very much on edge, and all the time aware of him – him and those violent muscles.

"Good, eh?" He glanced at her from under his lashes, fully aware of his physical power and what he could force her to do in response to him.

"Very good," she agreed, popping a carrot into her mouth and picturing the amazement of her friends in London if they could see her right now, clad like a *houri*, eating like an urchin, and companioned by a Berber in open-necked *kibr* and black *serwal*. It was all so fantastic, except that she could feel the brush of Zain's arm against hers, and with each breath the tang of Arabian coffee was in her nostrils. The copper lamps made a slight swaying motion on their chains, and the plaintive desert music still drifted in from the night, where the slim curve of the moon lay against the dense velvet of the sky.

"What are you thinking?"

She almost told him that she was visualising the incredulity of her old friends if they could see her with him. "Don't you know, El Zain?" she murmured. "I thought you were omnipotent."

"I think you are beginning to realise that you really are in my power, and I don't say it arrogantly, but because it happens to be a fact."

"Like – like some caveman carrying off a woman, is that it? You're a very primitive man, aren't you, El Zain?"

"Am I?" He shrugged his shoulders and the brown skin rippled under the neck slash of the *kibr*. "There is no place for weaklings in my kind of world, not that women need muscles – they have a magic of their own."

"Are you paying me an oblique compliment?" she dared to ask. "I thought I was just a mercenary creature who could be of use to you, and that beyond my possession of a female body I had no – no magic, as you call it."

"Yours is not of the obvious kind, and for the moment I don't take into account your physical beauty – ah yes, you know you have that so don't look at me as if I say the words in Arabic. That man to whom you were engaged must have been worthless trash to have broken with you on account of a mere limp . . . I wonder did you love him?"

"What is that to you?" It disturbed her, so that she had to hide her hands in a damask napkin in case he noticed that they were unsteady. She didn't want him to say things that got under her guard, and her skin. It was somehow easier to bear if he took her body without wanting the person as well. . . if he encroached on her personality then she would have no defence against him. He was a man of power, of a charisma that held together an entire desert tribe, and she was but a girl who had no one in the world.

"No, you had no real love for that stick of a man," he said, a decisive edge to each word. "It turned your head a little, eh, that a man from a titled family should ask you to be his wife?"

"It was bound to," she agreed. "I seem to have got into the habit of having my head turned by titles – look at yours! You know, I always believed that Eastern potentates spent their days and nights in idle luxury, surrounded by their houris. You've quite spoilt the picture for me."

"I thought I might have improved it." He leaned back against the cushions and slowly peeled an orange. "Softened by sensuality, Zahra, I would be of no use to my people. My chosen father, the Khalifa Hassan Hamid, entrusted them to me – I wonder, won't you grant me a virtue or two?"

"Oh, I don't doubt that in everything your people take precedence – look at me, my freedom is to be taken away because your tribe comes before my wishes, and your own. Would you marry again if it weren't a matter of solemn duty?"

He studied her in silence, and then he leaned forward and pressed a piece of orange between her lips. "You think too much, *bint*. It is time to do more feeling than thinking – here in the East we say that woman wasn't made to be wise like an old prophet, so remove that frown before it creases your white skin."

With her mouth full of orange Sarah couldn't make the reply she would have liked to make, not that anything she said made much impression on his tough hide.

"The Berber woman is taught from a small girl to be pleasing in the presence of a man." He smiled impudently. "It is no bad thing, for a woman to practise harmony instead of discord."

As he spoke she felt his eyes slipping over her hair and her robe of green *chartreuse*, vivid and silky against her white skin, with full sleeves that fell away at the bend of her elbow. "Don't look at me like that!" she wanted to cry out. Oh God, other men had looked and it had meant less than nothing – with him it was entirely different. His look, his touch, his slightest movement were a threat to her

142

peace of body and mind.

"Poor women of the East," she said, "when they aren't bowing down to the lordly male, they're carrying the burden of every petty fault in the book – not to mention a very serious blemish, such as being the mothers of men! Has it never occurred to you blameless males that you wouldn't be here to crow at all if it wasn't for some woman?"

"It never really ceases to occur to a man," he drawled, and his eyes were infinitely mocking as he allowed his meaning to sink into her mind, and her very nerves. "Come, aren't you going to eat the dessert that was specially prepared for you? You ate it with such delicate greed the last time we were together that I had Mehmed order it again for you – you see, I do what I can to tempt you."

As always she sensed a double meaning in his words; placed temptingly on a dish was the pomegranate crushed with cream and honey which had tasted heavenly the first time it was served to her, and there was a little silver spoon with which to eat the sweet. "I – I'd like to throw it in your arrogant face," she choked. "If that's what you mean by being tempted?"

"Throw it by all means," he invited. "Be a little gutter-snipe if that will ease your tensions, but it will be Mehmed who has to clean the mess off the divan, for I shall move very swiftly out of the way."

"You would!" She didn't have to be told that he was as resilient of movement as any feline; also his use of the word guttersnipe had struck at her sensibilities with cruel force. Meeting the slumbrous energy in his gaze, she hated him for being so completely his own master – and hers!

"Eat the sweet," he ordered. "Or I shall feed you like a *poussin*."

"I'm no baby hen, and if you think I'd let you – "

"Very well, shall we prove once more that I have the ability to force you into doing whatever I fancy to do?"

"I don't doubt the effectiveness of your brute strength," she said. "I've had examples of it!"

"Then pick up that spoon and eat your confection. That's right, delicious, is it not, and you were going to deprive yourself and your sweet tooth."

"Bully," she muttered, and all the time she ate the delectable sweet she stared at a curved scimitar attached to a far wall of the solarium; its blade looked scarifying enough to slice through armour let alone a throat. There were ibises and falcons flying in imagery in the panels of the walls . . . they were all part of the personality of the man beside her . . . this Berber chief who could exert over her an authority that was like iron. His dominance was absolute because she lacked the one thing that might make him vulnerable – she couldn't move his heart that lay out there in the desert with the girl whom he had called his joy.

"You shall be rewarded, *bebé*, for clearing your plate." He rose and went to a far table on which stood a box with that chased gazelle motif; he put back the lid and took something out of the box. It gleamed and shimmered on a chain and quite casually he threw it into her lap. It was a huge topaz that held the shifting gold colours of a desert sunrise, but Sarah sat and looked at it as if it were the eye of a snake.

"Put it around your throat," he ordered. "You know I don't have to tell you twice."

"Is it genuine?" She picked it up, gave the jewel a contemptuous look and dropped it to the floor. "I don't go in for fakes, thank you."

"If you don't pick that up at once, then you will learn that I don't go in for childish displays of pique. Pick it up!"

"What if I don't?" She leaned back against a cushion and gave him a mutinous look. "What will you do, your highness? Give me the traditional seven strokes of the whip for insubordination?"

"Believe me I'm tempted – though seven kisses might

144

subdue you rather more than any whipping. Now retrieve that chain and put it around your neck so I can see if the topaz suits you."

"I don't think I want it," she wondered at her own temerity in defying him, for his chin looked as adamant as clefted rock as he stood there looking down at her. "It probably belonged to some wretched woman who had it torn from her neck – "

"You have a vivid imagination, Zahra." He took a step towards her and her every nerve tightened itself for the coming conflict. "As a matter of fact I purchased that stone in a *souk* in the far south and I had it mounted with the idea of giving it to one of my young sisters. But somehow I hesitated because it seemed not to suit either of them – a kind of tawny tiger's eye with a flame at its centre, a red-gold one. Directly I saw your hair and your skin I knew that I wanted to see the topaz against your throat, so you will oblige me by wearing it – or do you prefer that I make you wear it?"

She hesitated as she saw the savage setting of his mouth and the movement of a vein beating at his temple . . . during that instant of hesitation he took a sudden stride across the room, a lean hand plucking up the chain as her nerves betrayed her and she cowered away from him.

When she did that he showed her the white edge of his teeth and the topaz hung glowing in front of her eyes. "I wanted you to have this as a kind of talisman against any harm in the desert, and you will have it whether you want it or not!" The next instant he was beside her and his hard arms were around her, holding her in a warm vice of flesh and muscle as he adjusted the chain about her neck so the gem settled in the hollow of her throat. Then he bent his head to her and crushed his lips to hers in a savage, bruising way, so that she gave a nervous shudder when he slackened his hold on her.

"What, I wonder, am I going to do with such a woman?"

he drawled, his lips a mere inch from her left ear so that she felt his warm breath close to her skin, and the weight of the topaz against the quick-beating pulse in her throat.

"I – I'm sure there isn't a doubt in your mind about what you're going to do with me," she said shakily. "I'm to bow to your every whim . . . run like your little bitch when you snap your fingers. I'm not to have a will of my own, am I?"

"My foolish one, I'm not out to break your spirit, but when a man gives a rather valuable gem to a woman it is understandable if he expects her to be pleased rather than insulting about the gift. As if," his hard fingers crept about her neck, "I would wish to see against your skin anything but a real live gem. Such skin, *bint,* like stroking one's fingers against the petals of the white lotus, smooth – ah, how smooth, with the tremor of your living warmth instead of the coolness of a flower that lives in beauty for such a short while. I like your spirit, but don't be quite a little shrew or I shall be forced to tame you."

She gazed up into the hard, almost fierce structure of his face, into the blue smouldering eyes.

"Women are the door of paradise on earth," he murmured, "so why fight it?"

"You're talking about desire – possession." The wild colour ran up into her skin, flushing over her cheekbones. "Do you think I like it, knowing I'm just an object that happens to please your eye – like this topaz you make me wear?"

"Would you prefer to be colourless, unnoticed, living in the grey shadows of life? Not you, Zahra. You put yourself on display like the dragonfly and you couldn't endure it when one of your dazzling attributes became damaged . . . you flew away from it all, straight into my net, as you think of it. Do I cast you off because you have a foot that is a little stiff? Do I not hold you to myself and wish to make a wife of you?"

"Anything female would do for what you want, El Zain. You must have a son, and I'm available and not exactly hideous!"

"*Ay*, a son." All at once his face became rather moody and his arms slid away from her. He leaned forward and took a cheroot from a box, and his black brows were drawn downwards as he struck a match and lit up. Smoke spiralled from his nostrils and he stared across the solarium as if seeing the ghosts of yesterday; the slim honeyed figure of Farah, who had left him to sleep for ever in the desert, and who hadn't lived to bear the agony of their son's dying.

Sarah's fingers crept to the topaz . . . was it remotely possible that she envied Farah for being loved so much? No one had loved her for herself, not for years, since Gran had died. Peter Jameson hadn't known the meaning of the word, and for El Zain she was just a pretty object to please him in the getting of a son. He was quite honest about it, at least. He hadn't lied and sworn he was in love with her. In that he had been far more honourable than her Englishman, and looking at him right now she recalled what Sheikh Moulay had said about a deeply felt grief, that time only stitched a thin skin over the wound and that it went on hurting regardless of all the duties, problems, and fleeting pleasures of a man's life.

Zain Hassan rose to his feet and walked to the far end of the solarium, where the *mesharabiya* let in the night air redolent of the far desert. He stood there in absolute stillness, like a figure carved from teak, hearing voices in the whisper of the sands, hearing his name on lips long silent.

His hand carried the cheroot to his lips and the smoke drifted to Sarah. "You can go to your own apartment," he said. "I won't detain you, but remember we shall be riding tomorrow. Mehmed will give you a call and bring riding garments for you."

147

Now there was a coolness to his voice that struck at Sarah, bringing her to her feet in an instant. "Good night," she said, and made for the door.

He gave a low throaty laugh. "You can't wait to leave me, can you? *Emshi besselma.*" He gave her a brief, sardonic bow and watched as she slipped out of the room, well aware that as she made her way to her tower room one of the silent-footed guards was in attendance. The winding stairs felt cold and she had again that feeling that she was the prisoner of a man's cold-hearted passion . . . some of it for her, but most of it for the Beni Zain. When she reached her door she turned and called out goodnight to Raschid; she knew it was he for he was always very formal and courteous, following her at a discreet distance, and one of those men whom she felt instinctively was a whole-hearted supporter of the Khalifa. She couldn't look to him for any sort of help in getting away from the *kasbah,* but she sometimes wondered if Daylis would help her.

Right now she was desperately tired and couldn't think about it, and once inside her room she allowed her shaken nerves to overcome her and she sank down full length on the ottoman and with hands clenched in the filmy covers she let all the fears and doubts and wonderments sweep over her. There was no way to forget that he had crushed her against the firm ribs that caged his savage heart, this man who held in his power an entire tribe of far from placid people. There was no way to brush away his touch, or wipe from her memory that feel of his hard cheek and the bold lips burning against hers.

She pressed her hand against her lips and in that mood of not being entirely her own person any more she tried to recall the face of Peter Jameson, the sound of his voice, the way he kissed and held her. But the memories were gone, wiped away as if they had never been, and so she knew how little there had been of love in that fleeting engagement.

If you had truly loved, then you didn't forget so easily. You could look down a vista of years, as Zain Hassan had looked, and the beloved faces were still as real as ever.

Oh God, it wasn't enough that she was being forced into marriage with a man who didn't love her . . . once married to him she would have to share his memory of a lovely Berber girl, who like his sisters would have had glistening black hair, a deep lustre to her eyes, expressive wrists and ankles weighted down with chains of gold, and she would have smiled as only a woman desperately desired could smile.

He wouldn't have made her do anything that she didn't want to do, and Sarah's mouth had a mutinous set to it as she sat up and removed the chain and topaz from around her neck. The large stone shimmered in the pool of her hand, admittedly very lovely but given merely as a token and not meant to convey any feelings of *tendresse*.

Was it worth a great deal? She studied its beautifully chiselled facets and thought again of Daylis and wondered if he could be bought, or if he was too certain of Zain Hassan's temper to dare to help a mere woman.

There was no escaping the Eastern attitude towards women . . . they were a pleasant garden in which to play, but it was foolish of a man to sell his soul to the devil for the sake of a woman. Sarah sighed and tossed the topaz among the toiletries on the dressing-table. She disrobed for bed and tried not to think about the morning, when again she was to have a lesson in being submissive to that tawny devil. She flung her red *babouches* across the room in a flash of temper, and taking up a hair brush she punished her hair with long hard strokes. It was a chore she didn't have to undertake, for she had only to ring the little hand bell beside her bed and her *fatima* would come running.

"I don't want someone waiting on me hand and foot," she had told the Khalifa. "I had enough of being helpless when I was in hospital."

"Please yourself," he had replied. "But the maid is always available when you require her assistance."

Damn him, he wasn't going to turn her into one of those lolling, lazy creatures who wouldn't move to fetch a magazine from a table. His sister Lallou was inclined to be this way and already, at eighteen, she was far plumper than she should be. She was to have been married the previous year, but her fiancé had been killed in some kind of desert fracas, and she seemed to spend most of her time curled up on a divan, stuffing herself with honey tarts and pieces of jelly stuffed with nuts, her nose buried in French and American magazines.

Sarah was inclined to prefer Belkis, a pretty name meaning honey girl, which suited her, for she was very charming, with the huge brown eyes of a doe and skin like honey-silk. She was almost seventeen, and it sometimes seemed to Sarah that her youthful pleasure in life was shot through by a certain apprehension. Their brother was responsible for planning their lives and choosing their husbands, and Sarah was inclined to wonder if Belkis rebelled against being forced into marriage with a man she might not meet until the actual ceremony. It was a barbaric way of introducing a young girl to the facts of life, throwing her like that into the arms of a stranger. No wonder Belkis had a little shadow in her eyes, as if she were haunted by that coming event in her life.

As she herself was haunted, Sarah thought, as she climbed into bed and drew around her the filmy netting that kept out any winged intruders. She had also been told very forcibly to always shake out her shoes before putting them on in the mornings, for scorpions and spiders had a nasty habit of creeping into dark apertures.

She curled down in the ottoman and felt against her feet the bed warmer that was necessary at night, and she felt very alone in her tower even though she knew that she had only to touch that hand bell at the bedside and someone would arrive within minutes to attend to her slightest want.

The soft moonlight stole through the carved woodwork at her windows, reminding her yet again that only a matter of days separated her from the ceremony that would end her own independence for good. When the great musk moon of the desert was at its zenith, she would no longer lie alone in bed at night . . . she would sleep in those hard brown arms that would hold every inch of her to that vital body and make her part of his strange Berber world.

Sarah buried her face in her pillows and felt her toes curling in silent torment against the bed warmer. There seemed no way out for her . . . she was as much in his power as his sisters, and his power in this part of the world was absolute, and no doubt relentless towards anyone who interfered in that most personal part of his life, his *serayi*, for in that private section lived his women, and to the men of the East women remained creatures of strange and enticing secrets that had to be guarded.

With a restless movement Sarah turned over in her ottoman bed and felt the movement of softest silk against her skin. In her nostrils was the subtle perfume which pervaded her room . . . it seemed already that she was no longer Sarah Innocence but the *kadin* of a ruthless Berber chief who had re-named her Zahra, a girl of the West who was to be gradually absorbed into the life of the East . . . wife of Zain Hassan bin Hamid and prospective mother of his children.

She lay there in the milky darkness, staring up at the pyramid of netting, seeing his face and those incredible blue eyes blotting out everything as his mouth possessed hers and his arms bound her to his lithe brown body. The recollection was vivid and physical, and Sarah felt as if a live current had shot its way through her bones, so that she tingled and went suddenly hot all over.

No . . . she flung herself on her face again and wanted it

all blotted out in the depths of sleep. *"Abide with me,"* she whispered, *"fast falls the eventide."* Never in her life had she felt so alone and so afraid . . . it wasn't a physical fear, but it seemed to be linked to what lay in his past, not to what lay in her future.

The night wind whispered beyond the *mesharabiya* . . . countless grains of sand rustling on the sides of the dunes as they curved up to meet the crescent moon, and the sad ghost that walked there left no footmarks in the lonely desert.

Sarah woke abruptly and saw a slim brown hand moving aside the bed netting. Her *fatima* smiled and held a cup of coffee towards her, and blinking sleepily she sat up to take it. As she sat sipping the hot sweet brew the maid placed some garments on the bed . . . the riding things that she was to wear. Her heart tightened. He was going to make her ride with him, and he knew she'd be sick with panic.

"Stay," she said to the girl, who understood a few words of English. "I shall need help with these." She indicated the clothes and the girl nodded, going across to the washing alcove to pour water into the big copper bowl.

Half an hour later Sarah was clad in the cloth trousers that hugged her legs, a jerkin of softest suede, supple boots to match, and a white linen *shesh* bound around her hair. The maid handed her a short braided whip and her fingers clenched it as she stared at herself in the mirror.

"Well, Analita, do I look anything like a Berber woman?" she asked, and saw a wry little smile form on her own lips.

Her *fatima* gave a shake of her head and placed her hands together as she studied Sarah. "The *sitt* like a boy – very pretty boy."

"That will please his lordship," Sarah said drily, and she

whacked her whip against her Berber pants and felt the agitation of her nerves, and the fear of riding that she was trying to hold down. What was Zain Hassan after? Did he want to see her on horseback, or did he wish to have her grovelling at his knees, begging that he spare her? She stood there tensely as it swept over her again, the way Grey Lady had dashed off at a furious gallop, half throwing Sarah out of the stirrups so that she had no defence, no strength to match against the mare when she plunged wildly into that copse and maddened by the slash of the branches had flung Sarah clear out of the saddle and headlong into the harsh trunk of a tree, her left foot twisting grotesquely as she landed on the ground.

No, I can't do it, she thought wildly, but Mehmed had arrived to take her to the Khalifa and in a mood of doom she found herself walking down the spiral stairs in the wake of the manservant. Damn Zain Hassan! He was testing her nerve, not trying to effect a cure for her fear of horses; fearless himself he had only contempt for it in other people, and she was the woman he had selected to be the bearer of his son. Sarah flung up her head, tendrils of her red hair bright against the whiteness of the *shesh*, its intricate binding completed by a scarf that hung down over her shoulder. She'd show him that she wasn't quite as lily-livered as he expected to find her. She'd climb on that horse even if she was in a blue funk, and she certainly wouldn't give the lord and master the satisfaction of tossing her into the saddle.

She followed Mehmed across a courtyard that was silent and cool, so early was it, with the tiny coloured birds just beginning to hop out of the pepper trees. They walked beneath a great stone archway out upon a pavement where at once she caught the sound of hooves ringing on the stones as a pair of superb black horses were led into view. They wore saddles of scarlet and a single glance was enough to tell Sarah that they were of pure desert blood, their coats like black satin, their manes long and thick along necks that were beautifully arched. As they were led forward on strong and elegant legs they strained against the bit, snuffing the air, great tails arching. One of them was led by a stable hand, but the other was in the charge of Zain Hassan himself, as always in cloak and head-robe looking more haughty, more falcon-faced, more than ever the Berber chief who was unbelievably the son of a soldier who himself had been born on the bar sinister side of a noble family.

Catching the flash of those blue eyes beneath the white head-robe, Sarah stiffened, as if to attention like a raw recruit who was about to be battle tested. His eyes swept her up and down and she expected that mocking smile to play on his lips, but instead he gave a slight nod of satisfaction.

"You suit the clothes and they suit you," he said. "Good morning, Zahra, I hope you are looking forward to our ride?"

"Good morning, El Zain," she replied, in a cool tone of voice. "Is that my mount, the one you're holding by the reins?"

He inclined his head and into his eyes stole a faint smile. "And she says it so coolly," he drawled. "You would go like that to the firing squad, eh, with your chin in the air and your green eyes hating the enemy – in this instance I am the enemy and well aware of it. Your mount is a filly and her name in English is Firebird. She has a winged grace and a gracious disposition and is rather better trained than the mare that ran away with you. Come, fondle her nose, let her get the scent of you and the feel of you. Come!"

It was a distinct order, and Sarah could feel the tremor in her legs and the way her limp was more pronounced as she forced herself to approach the shining, elegant horse. Her heart beat somewhere in her throat and with her every instinct she wanted to cower away from the thoroughbred and the man who held her reins twisted around his brown fingers. That alone was enough to tell Sarah that the filly was spirited and eager to be off into the desert.

"At least," Sarah swallowed the dryness from her throat, "I shan't take such a wallop on the sands."

"You aren't going to be thrown this time," he said firmly. "Come to the horse, touch her and make friends."

"I – I can't," Sarah backed away and didn't notice that she went in the direction of the black stallion which the stablehand was holding. He reared up and Sarah turned in time to see the long legs coming down upon her . . . she stood there petrified, and then felt the thrust of a hand that sent her sprawling out of the way as the stallion was eased down and pulled to one side.

Hands reached down for Sarah and pulled her upright. Those same hands shook her and looking up at him, half shocked and half scared, she saw his eyes cutting into her like steel.

"Are you asking for a broken neck?" he demanded. "Perhaps it was over-optimistic of me to expect sensible behaviour from such as you."

"Such as I?" Temper took the place of fright and Sarah's eyes blazed into his. "A fool of an English girl who walked into your trap and can't find a way out. I might yet find one! While there's time there has to be hope of getting out of your clutches!"

"Time?" he jeered softly. "Here in the desert there is all the time in the world, for the place is eternal and will stay that way until the very end of time. Come, are the nerves gathered together again?"

"Oh, let go of me," she shook him off with surprising ease, not noticing that he had deliberately slackened his hold on her. "I'll show you and yours if I'm such a white-skinned fool!" Strung up to a pitch of that bravado which had brought her to this outlandish place, Sarah went over to Firebird, who was snuffling at a nearby shrub, caught at her reins, set her foot in the stirrup and mounted into the scarlet saddle with an easy swing of her slim body, once so beautifully coordinated before the damage to her ankle. God, how it came back to her, the grace and flexibility of her own body in the saddle, for here it didn't show, couldn't be seen that her left foot, gripped now by the stirrup, was a trifle stiff when she walked.

She sat there a moment, a little stunned that she had dared to do this, and then with a sudden husky laugh she leaned forward and stroked the horse's satiny neck.

"Bravo!" There was a swirl of the great cloak as Zain Hassan swung into the saddle of his stallion. "What a son we shall have between us, Zahra! Turquoise-eyed, reckless with his tongue and his courage; proud, obstinate and gallant."

Gallant . . . it was a word that went through her, for she knew he referred to what she had just done in overcoming her fear of being thrown again.

"Ah yes," he softly laughed, "the British are so gallant, are they not?"

"You should know," she rejoined.

"Should I?" His blue eyes raked over her, taking in with expert judgment the way she sat the high-bred Berber horse, hands light yet firm on the leather reins, knees close in against the sleek sides of the animal, slim shoulders held straight without making a ramrod of her spine. Peter Jameson had called hers a good riding seat, but at that time it had been a natural part of her work as a model; she had possessed a flair for using her lissom body, in and out of the water, on a bike or the back of a horse.

Now it mattered more, for she had overcome reluctance and the spectre of pain, driven to it by a dozen different emotions associated with the man who rode beside her. How different he looked from her faint memory of Peter, clad like that in *kibr* and cloak; big, strong, incredibly at ease in his manhood.

Now the cloistered path narrowed and he rode ahead of her, that tan-coloured cloak spread upon the hindquarters of his horse. A boy from him, turquoise-eyed! That strange, prickling current ran through Sarah's bones ... of course, the blue and the green of their eyes blending like the sea into aquamarine.

She tried to wrench her thoughts from him, feeling the elegant movements of Firebird beneath her, the well-shod hooves striking on stone and then suddenly softened as if upon velvet as the shady cloisters parted to let them into the desert from the rear of the *kasbah*. Sarah caught her breath, for the dawn sky over the sands was a flush of wild apricot, turning them to a tawny gold that later on the sun would burn into a shimmering haze that pained the eyes.

"Beautiful!" The word escaped from Sarah, and the robed head of Zain Hassan turned as he caught her exclamation and he gazed a moment at the way she was looking at the sea of shimmering sand lit by the pale turquoise and gold of the early morning sky. It was somehow unearthly in its sense of freedom and purity, with beyond those veils of turquoise a curve of softest flame – the rising sun.

"A deceptive beauty, Zahra. In about an hour all of this will have changed and that was why I wanted you to know what it feels like to ride in a dawn mirage. I am glad you are appreciative."

She caught the dry note in his voice, but the look she gave him was one of curiosity. "I thought the desert had every virtue in your eyes, El Zain, but now you call it a deceiver."

"Which it is." He eased the stride of his stallion so that their mounts were loping side by side. "The desert is as unpredictable as a tiger – or a woman. Sometimes as now it is awesome in its loveliness, but at other times it takes on claws that rend the nerves when the wind rises and the sands are let loose to make nightmare for any rider caught in a *khamsin*. It is sheer hell when great clouds of dust darken the face of the sun and a sultry heat falls like a stifling blanket over the nostrils and the mouth and one's skin becomes caked with sand grains. Then the fearful winds will blow away and the night is filled with burning stars and strange primal vibrations seem to be in the very air and one breathes deeply of the countless scents let loose in this timeless land – then, my *bint*, the desert is sheer magic."

As he lifted his face to the sun that had not yet become a flaming disc that could injure the naked eye, Sarah felt that he worshipped this golden land in every fibre of his body. He might call it a tiger, but he would never be afraid of it. He might regard its changes of mood as being like those of a woman, but he would never be less than tolerant because he loved the place. He had a basic, passionate interest in this vital infinity of space, where the fantastic rocks were seamed with strange crystals, and where in their shade grew the few flowers and shrubs.

The desert wasn't barren, even though the flowers lasted but a day or so and then were shrivelled into dust by the scorching sun. Nor was it silent, for there seemed to be a far-off keening all the time, as if lost souls wandered among the sand towers and sinister crevices, and those sudden remains of mud walls, broken doorways and palm fronds making a screen of shadows.

"Are you not going to ask why I sometimes find the desert like a woman?"

Sarah glanced sideways at Zain Hassan and she saw the amusement in his eyes and the glint of curiosity, as if he had expected her to refute his statement that an awesome place of sand dunes and sun-cracked rocks could be anything like a female, who to all outward appearances was soft, smooth and pliant.

"The desert has a temper," she said. "It can look

inviting and then suddenly turn nasty. I'm not a fool, El Zain. I know that women are creatures of extremes."

"They love or they hate, eh? They smile or they claw."

"But that doesn't mean that men are saints, by a long piece of chalk!" Sarah tossed her head and the scarf of her *shesh* lifted in a little gust of wind.

She heard him laugh in his throat. "What eyes you have, Zahra. Beautiful as a field of mint, which is a very fine compliment in the East."

"Don't your people also say that when the tongue drips with honey it is getting ready to sting?" But she had flushed slightly at his remark and found that she rather liked it for its poetic quality. What was he doing? Was he courting her just a little, and making her like it . . . as Peter had with his insincere flattery and his shallow-hearted talk about cherishing her.

This time memory was sharp and stabbing, and she gave the man at her side a sudden cold look. "I prefer you when you're candid and stinging, El Zain. I don't trust you when you try to beguile me with soft talk – it's just another game with you, and I'm not quite a fool that I don't know when I'm being seduced, even if you do happen to be a master at it!"

"Ah, how suspicious of you, Zahra, and I thought that we might be establishing some sort of rapport here in the desert." The mockery stole back into his eyes, that beneath the head-robe and its ropes were bluer and yet more elongated; more definitely eyes of the East, letting her see the desert forces in him transmitted from the Berber girl who had given birth to him.

"I could never have any real rapport with you," she flared. "As I accept that I am British, you accept that you are Eastern, and there is no real meeting place even if your –" She broke off, remembering that she had been warned never to mention his father. "Never the twain shall meet, isn't that what they say?"

"Do they?" He lifted his braided whip and gestured all around them. "Yet here we are, Zahra, you and I. The East and the West have met, and not for the first time, eh? So you have asked questions about me and had them answered – it was inevitable, but it is something I don't discuss and I don't intend to break that rule, even with you. I am part of this world and shall remain so all my life; part of all that is fascinating, cruel and elemental, like the hawks that fly in that sky above us, like the palms that sink their roots into the rock itself, like the eagles that smash open tortoises on the stones and consume the hearts inside."

He gazed beyond her into the heart of the desert, and up towards the hills that curved like a monstrous spine, bordered by tamarisk with its roots in the hanging rock. The desert winds, the burning sun, the coldness at night, these made the people equally hard, weathered and picturesque.

As Zain Hassan sat there on his black horse, his cloak billowing from his shoulders, there could be no denying that he had a certain noble air about him. His profile held a pride that made her catch her breath, strong and definite as bronze rather than flesh, the deep lines of authority already stamped hard in his face.

He could never be vulnerable, for long ago in early boyhood he had been taught not to cry when he hurt himself; drilled not to bow down to weariness or grief, until he hardened into a man to whom others could turn in their hurt and angers and grief. If when Farah had died those blue eyes had ached with tears, no one would have seen them . . . he would, Sarah knew it instinctively, have come here to the desert to be consoled.

"I can see that you belong to all this," she said, "that it's the most important aspect of your life to be of the desert, and a man of power who can control tribal matters and put down rebellions. But have you thought of me at all? Have you considered me as a *person*?"

He turned his gaze from the desert to look at her. "I can consider you only as a woman," he replied. "If that sounds arrogant, then so be it. When I saw your photograph I wanted to meet you, and you might well have turned out to be a painted doll who giggled and had no mind of your own, and then I should have sent you packing. But you have spirit and I like that. The desert won't worry you, once you have become used to its moods. It has infinite variety – as you have, *hilwa*."

He smiled, his teeth firm and white against his tawny skin. "Think of you as a person? I can only think of you as Saiyida Zahra, which translated into your tongue means Princess Sarah."

Her heart seemed to turn over when he said that . . . it was incredibly true that marriage to Zain Hassan would elevate her to that position . . . when she became his wife she automatically became a Moroccan princess. In place of that glass slipper which Peter Jameson had held out, she was now offered a golden one, and she was afraid of it.

"I – I don't think I shall make a very good wife," she said. "If we had anything in common it might be different, but you were brought up to rule and I was brought up in a working class area of London. I'm no lady –"

"A lady, Zahra, is a woman of infinite respect for herself as a human being, making her way in life without making a commodity of her body, or her principles."

"Yet you called me mercenary," she reminded him. "That surely implies that I care only about the material things in life? If that were so, then I'd grab at you, with your riches and your power!"

"Instead," he mocked, "you want to run away from me. You'd have done better to have played the greedy little tart, Zahra, for then I should have assisted you out of Morocco without any argument at all. When I called you

mercenary I challenged you to show me that you were . . .
instead you fought with me and threw a very valuable
gem at my feet. Your fate was sealed from that moment."

"My fate?" she echoed. "Meaning that you'll force me
into this marriage whatever my feelings?"

"Meaning precisely that, my *bint*." His eyes held hers,
glintingly. "It's no unusual thing in this part of the world,
for women can be as nervy and high-strung as an un-
trained filly, and they have a tendency to jib away from
the hand of authority. Better to have a master who knows
his mind than a fool who is all mouth and weak knees.
You had a dose of that, eh? It wasn't much fun, was it,
when it came to the harsh realities. But I made you mount
a horse and I made you ride again – has the experience
been so unenjoyable?"

Sarah looked around her in a hunted way . . . he had her
in a corner again, trapped by his iron-clad logic and his
determination.

"I shouldn't," he softly drawled. "I can very easily ride
you down, and let me warn you that if you eluded me, there
are rogue bedouins in the desert who can be most dis-
courteous. Would you prefer their hands to mine?"

Her gaze fell to his hands on the reins of his stallion,
lean and brown and incredibly strong, and also im-
peccably clean. She remembered the feel of them on her
skin, mastering her struggles and yet leaving not a mark
on her arms, her neck, wherever he had touched her with
the skill of an experienced lover.

That burning sensation ran over her body, and then she
quivered as something struck her face . . . a cold sliver of
wetness from out of the sky.

"Is it going to rain?" she exclaimed, touching her cheek
where the cool wetness was a little like a teardrop.

"As I told you, Zahra, the desert can be unpredictable."
As he glanced at the sky a sudden soundless flicker of
lightning made his horse start up, pawing the air for a

moment like a sculpture against the storm-gold sky.
"We will make our way back before it really comes down
hard."

"Oh, I don't mind the rain," she laughed. "I'm English
and I'm used to getting wet."

"You have never been caught in a desert rainpour.
It can soak you to the skin in a matter of moments, so now
we really ride, *bébé*, and you will feel the speed in the sinews
of Firebird, and you will not be afraid, eh?"

His eyes locked with hers, blue and steely as the lightning
in the sky, and then they were off and nothing had ever
been more exhilarating than that gallop across the sands
as the rain fell faster every minute and there flickered all
around them those slivers of white-hot light, like knives
being struck across the rocks. Zain's great cloak blew in
the wind, and the scarf of Sarah's *shesh* thrashed back
and forth across her mouth, and the strange part was that
she was quite unafraid and even felt a smile on her rain
stung lips.

When they came within sight of the *kasbah* walls she
felt a pang that their wild ride was almost ended. Who
would have believed it, that she would lose entirely
her fear of a horse let loose in a gallop, but this beautiful
creature was perfectly trained and obedient to the slightest
command from her rider, even with the rain pelting her
black coat and with thunder growling from the hills.

They cantered in under the great archway and there
they halted for a breathless moment. Sarah's eyes were
brilliantly green as they met her companion's, and the
next instant she felt a stab under her ribs as she saw the
look on his face . . . the dark, drawn look through the
mask of rain.

"I hate storms," he growled.

"I thought it was rather exciting," she dragged off her
rain-soaked *shesh* and shook free her red hair.

He stared at her and never had she seen his eyes look

so dense a blue, so shadowed in his hard-boned face; a raindrop ran down his cheek and she watched as it melted into his skin.

"My son died as it thundered out there." He gestured with his whip and his knuckles were bone-white as he gripped the braided leather. "I can't abide the sound!"

Then, wheeling his horse, he rode on ahead of her in the direction of the stables. Sarah followed, uncaring of the rain on her hair, listening as the water splashed down on the stones of the courtyard, wincing now as the voice of the storm growled across those desert spaces.

The heavens themselves blaze forth the death of princes . . . right now Sarah felt strongly the need in Zain Hassan to have another son. In order to satisfy that need he had to have Sarah, and just as he had made her ride . . . she caught her breath and tasted the rain on her mouth. Would she revel in submission to him as she had revelled in riding in his desert, knowing as she did that somewhere out there, under that stormy sky, lay the woman to whom he had given his heart.

The Berber girl who had died in giving him a child of love . . . now, suddenly, the rain felt cold and the steely flickers of lighting were somehow lethal, and she urged Firebird towards the stables. Zain Hassan had handed over his stallion to its groom and gone on his way into the *kasbah*.

It came as a relief, and yet at the same time Sarah felt a flick of disappointment that he had gone off to breakfast alone in readiness for his daily routine of dealing with tribal business . . . it was no use fooling herself that she was going to share everything with this complex man. He wanted her for a single basic reason, and he had made her ride again because it irritated him that she should fear anything. She was marked out to bear his son, and despite herself she had allowed him to find out this morning that she had courage. He liked that. It could make his eyes burn like flames, sweeping over her, engulfing her in passions that would get him what he wanted while destroying what lay in Sarah's heart.

The hope of love that lay in every woman's heart.

CHAPTER EIGHT

SARAH never doubted for a moment that Zain Hassan had his hands full with being the Khalifa, for despite a very efficient staff of advisers, bookkeepers and secretaries, it was he who had the final say in the decisions which had to be taken, sometimes domestic and at other times political. On his shoulders rested the welfare of the Beni Zain, financially, politically, and emotionally. Each man was entitled to bring his problems to the leader and he dealt with them personally.

It was from his sister Belkis that Sarah had learned all this, for she was more interested in things outside the *serayi* than her sister Lallou.

Having handed Firebird to a stable lad, Sarah made her way to the apartment which the sisters shared. Now and again she took a meal with them, and this morning she felt a need to get away from her own troubled thoughts, and she entered their sitting-room as morning coffee was being served.

"What good timing, may I join you?" she asked, hesitating a moment just inside the door, the unwound *shesh* trailing from her hand, and her hair in rain darkened strands about her shoulders.

Belkis gave her a startled look, sweeping her eyes up and down the boyish figure in jerkin, tight pants and boots. "I almost didn't recognize you, Zahra." Both girls spoke English, having been taught by Sheikh Moulay at their brother's suggestion, but they had adopted the Berber translation of her name as if in no doubt that she would be joining their household on a permanent basis.

"You look like a young Rif rider," Lallou said in her rich, lazy voice. "So our brother has made you go riding with him – I knew he would though you swore that he wouldn't make you do anything against your will. He is the grand master. He can show mercy, or order an execution if he so wishes. Did he inform you that he will be doing exactly that in about an hour's time?"

"What do you mean, Lallou?" Sarah sat down on a divan and accepted a cup of coffee and a crisp doughnut filled with damson jam.

"Don't let us talk about anything nasty," Belkis pleaded. "I want Zahra to tell me some more about London –"

But Sarah was staring at Lallou, sensing in what she had said something rather awful. "Your brother never talks to me of matters relating to the Beni Zain and he certainly made no mention of – of any execution. What do you mean, Lallou? Oh you can't mean – ?"

"But I do." A plump hand dunked a doughnut in hot coffee and the large, brown, rather mocking eyes of the slightly older sister were fixed upon Sarah's face. "A tribesman has been found guilty of knifing a neighbour and my brother must either have him executed or bring down the wrath of the neighbour's family on his own head. If he doesn't have the killer duly despatched, then he will let loose a blood feud, and that will mean more killings. Ah, don't look so shocked, Zahra. This is the East and here we abide by an eye for an eye."

"How –" Sarah swallowed. "How will the man be executed?"

"He must go by way of the blade, the way he killed his neighbour." And as she spoke, with cool greed, the Berber girl ate her soggy doughnut and though there was no real hostility in the way she regarded Sarah, she made it plain that she thought the English girl soft and too easily shocked.

"It will be swift." Belkis reached over and pressed Sarah's hand. "I know things are different in your country, but here our laws must suit our surroundings or, as my brother would tell you, there would be anarchy."

"In more earthy language, Zahra, we are a hot-blooded people." Lallou smiled slowly, showing her perfect teeth that her fondness for sweet things had not yet damaged. "You are of the West and you can view these matters more coolly, and you also have big prisons where offenders can be sent."

"Why," Belkis demanded of her sister, "did you have to mention any of this? Zahra would have been no wiser, and now she will think that Zain Hassan is cruel."

"Oh, I've never doubted that he can be cruel," Sarah said, and because she had gone cold at the thought of what he would soon set in motion she sipped at her coffee in order to warm herself again. "You both know that he keeps me here against my wishes, but being a woman I'm supposed to be flattered."

"Aren't you?" Lallou mocked. "Deep down in yourself, where we are all women under the skin, and where different colours of skin and ideologies have no place? Zain Hassan is a striking man, with immense power, and he has had to overcome hostility from certain of the caids in order to arrange his marriage to you. They would like him to marry again a Moslem woman; one who would know her proper place in his life and not expect the considerations that will be included in the marriage contract drawn up for your benefit."

"I want no marriage – no benefits," Sarah rejoined. "I want my freedom, that's all. I want to be allowed to go back to my own country, even if I will be poor and obscure. I didn't know where I was well off!"

"The silly girl is afraid of him," Lallou laughed softly, her plump feet curled among cushions, hoop earrings swinging against her cheeks, a dusting of *kohl* around her large eyes. "Look at us, do we weep because he has control of our lives? He doesn't use his horsewhip on women – nor, indeed, on his horses. Think yourself lucky!

You at least know the man who will in due course take you to bed, but my sister and I are in the dark. Better in the dark, perhaps, if some greybeard is chosen!"

"Don't say that," Belkis gasped. "You know I can't bear it!" She flung her hands over her ears, the collection of bangles sliding down her coffee-coloured arms. Sarah gave her a quick, sympathetic look, and thought again that Belkis secretly rebelled against the idea of being married off to a man chosen by her brother; someone she might hate at sight and yet have to live with. He was barbaric under that suave manner he could assume when it pleased him to do so, donning it like that picturesque cloak that he slung about his shoulders!

"If he's a greybeard, he'll be rich, which is something," Lallou shrugged and reached for another tidbit; a stick of celery stuffed with cream cheese. "What is marriage, after all, but another form of being protected, looked after, well fed? One has babies, that is all, and I shouldn't mind that. It's a small price to pay for security. You see, Zahra, we place a higher value on being secure than you women of the West. Do you really wish to go through life without a man to shoulder all the bothersome things?"

"Perhaps I don't wish to go through life – unloved." As Sarah put it into words she felt the flush that swept over her face. If it sounded old-fashioned she didn't much care; perhaps she had always been that kind of a girl even when she had been part of the go-getting, highly competitive and racy world of modelling? Perhaps deep in her heart she had always longed for what seemed the unreachable goal . . . that strange emotion that struck so suddenly, so forcibly, opening up the heart so that one person could step right inside and ever afterwards be part of your body and soul.

"Zahra!" Lallou gave a peal of laughter. "There will surely be plenty of that, for Zain is much of a man, and it is no secret why he is marrying again. If the tribal elders had had their way, it would have been sooner and with a woman of their choosing, but you know of course that our brother was deeply involved with his first wife. It took time for him to get over that, for the grief was redoubled when their child died. It was as if she beckoned one of them to follow her, was it not? But Zain Hassan is too tenacious of life, too strong and too necessary to his people to go like that at the behest of a woman, even one who adored him, almost worshipped his very shadow upon the sands, and he casts a long and very impressive shadow, does the Khalifa of Beni Zain."

Lallou lay back against her cushions and the kohled lids of her eyes drooped lazily as she watched Sarah, and yet behind those eyelids there seemed to be bright pinpoints of curiosity, as if this stepsister of Zain's would dearly like to know if Sarah was envious in any way of that close relationship which had marked the Khalifa's first marriage.

"Is that what you mean by love, Zahra?" she murmured. "That you would like to replace Farah in his heart and be to him what she was?"

"No," Sarah denied. "I am *me*, not some adoring slave who walked in his shadow. No doubt that would appeal to him, to have someone living, breathing, *being* just for him!"

"But that's exactly what love is, surely?" Lallou stroked with her fingertips the embroidery of a cushion, while Belkis had risen to her feet and wandered to an archway that led out to their private *zariba*. There the younger sister stood in her flowered dress slashed at the neck, worn over tight-fitting pantaloons. Sarah could see one of her slender hands clenching the ironwork inset into the archway, the young shoulders tensed as she listened to the conversation and kept her eyes averted . . . was it in case her pretty, soft-skinned face revealed an emotion that it shouldn't?

Sarah glanced at her wristwatch, which the old man who

went round daily winding all the clocks in the *kasbah* had mended for her, removing carefully the grains of sand which had clogged the minute workings. Her heart seemed to jar in her side and her green eyes filled with a kind of horror as she thought of what was happening right now, in some other part of this stone fortress.

Tall, cloaked, with a face of brown stone, Zain Hassan would be watching the execution of a murderer . . . Sarah felt as if drops of ice ran down her spine and she shivered so hard that she knocked from the edge of the divan table the cup and saucer from which she had been drinking. They fell to the carpet and the coffee dregs seeped into the thick wool . . . like blood, she thought, staining the stones where that man would have fallen.

"I can't – I won't stay here!" She jumped to her feet and looked about her like a trapped creature. "Won't someone help me – isn't there anyone who would risk it?"

"Risk the judgment that you know he can pass on to – offenders?" murmured Lallou, while Belkis spun round from the archway and stared at Sarah with frightened brown eyes.

"He'll never let you go," Belkis cried out. "The *serayi* is sacred from outsiders and the punishment would be awful – if the man was caught!"

The great brown eyes seemed to fill that oval-shaped face, and the tiny ringlets of hair curled in front of the small ears seemed night-black against the ashen skin. Sarah saw at once that Belkis was frightened and distressed on her own account, and this realisation helped to steady and slow down the sense of panic which had struck at Sarah. She breathed deeply and it slowly receded. Lallou was right, she couldn't expect anyone to take the risk of offending Zain Hassan, high lord and chief executioner of Beni Zain – master of the sword! Today, perhaps only moments ago, a sword had been used, and Sarah shrank from the moment when she saw him again – and was touched by him, for that blade had fallen at a gesture from one of his lean hands, so scrupulously scrubbed, and so ruthlessly efficient.

Sensing that Belkis had some inner trouble of her own, Sarah went to her and put an arm around her tense figure. "I'm sorry I unnerved you," she said, for she also sensed that Belkis wouldn't speak of her trouble in front of Lallou, who was obviously too loyal to Zain Hassan to be trusted not to repeat anything that she considered he ought to know. It was there in her eyes right now, a half-mocking threat directed at Sarah, who said at once:

"Go ahead and tell him everything I've said, Lallou. But you'll be talking to the air because he already knows how I feel about him. I don't mince my words with him. He knows that I'd run away if I had the chance."

"Then what a fool you are," Lallou said, with abrupt contempt. "My brother could have any one of a hundred women, and why he should choose you is a mystery – one which probably lies in his genes! We are not allowed to talk about *that*, but no doubt you have seen for yourself that he is not totally Berber. Blood calls to blood, so they say, and you have that white skin and that hair like flames against the milky colour of you. And you also have that halting foot, which in the eyes of some men would be a blemish. Think yourself lucky, *roumia*."

"You are being a cat, Lallou." Belkis looked at Sarah with apology in her eyes. "Take no notice of her, Zahra. She is jealous because Zain is going to be married, but I am pleased. I want you for a sister. I think you are kind and lovely, and I am sorry she told you about that awful thing which Zain has had to do. In time you will come to an understanding of our ways."

"It could take a lifetime," Sarah said, with a catch of her breath.

"Or a wedding night," Lallou murmured, watching

172

Sarah as she bit into the side of a ripe peach, the tip of her tongue licking the juice from the corners of her mouth.

"Lallou, why must you talk like that?" Belkis gave the indolent figure of her sister a flushed look. "You have no regard for the fact that Zahra might be shy, and you're always eating! Soon you will be as big as a camel."

"Watch your tongue that it doesn't become crabbed," Lallou rejoined. "Men like a voice of honey not one of vinegar. I really don't know what has come over you of late and I wonder if perhaps it shouldn't be whispered in Zain Hassan's ear that a husband be found for you before you become too sharp and jumpy."

"You will keep your suggestions to yourself," Belkis said, with a flash of temper. "You are the one who should ask for a husband before you swell out of all proportion from all those sweets and cakes that disappear inside your mouth all day long."

"What will it matter, little sister? It is the full moon that our men admire, not the thin crescent that keeps itself in veils, like a girl hiding in a corner, all knees and elbows and skittish fears." The mocking, almond eyes slipped over Sarah from her hair to her heels. "Be wise and please Zain Hassan, or you will make enemies among the Beni Zain. They will blame you not him if the marriage is a failure, for I understand that in the contract he is waiving his right to other wives and as a practising Moslem he is entitled to three. You know that, eh? The elders maintain that with his full quota of wives he could then be the father of a number of children – how many will he get from you, a woman from the cool shores of England? You see, you shrink away from the very mention of the subject!"

Sarah could feel herself in actual physical retreat from what Lallou was saying . . . she could feel the urge to press her hands over her ears in an attempt to shut it all out. She was a person, not a mere biological reason for being here; her every action watched and commented upon, her skin, hair and shape discussed as if they were the points of a filly who was soon to be serviced by the prize stallion!

"I – I haven't asked Zain Hassan to give up his right to Moslem wives," she said, in a half-choked voice. "I've said myself that he'd be better off with a Berber girl – he only wants me because I'm so different from Farah and can never remind him of how much he cared for her and how much he grieved when he lost her. I know his reasons for choosing me, and though they might seem reasonable to him, they just seem totally unfair to me. I'm just a female, and upon his shoulders rests the responsibility of marrying again – he doesn't really want to, but duty comes before everything else, and he thinks that by giving me a nice fat dowry I shall be content to fulfil all his demands. God, he makes me feel like a slave! Don't you understand that, Lallou? He takes away my independence and thinks that his gold will pay me back, and I don't get that until the priest has tied the knot and the silver sword has struck seven times at the door of our wedding chamber. Oh, I know the procedures from Sheikh Moulay, but I don't know how I shall endure them without screaming for help – I feel like the girl in the story who felt herself being entombed brick by brick and knew there wasn't a soul who cared that she screamed until the last brick choked her."

"Oh, you mustn't talk like that," Belkis gasped. "Are you so unhappy, Zahra? Do you hate our brother that much?"

"I hate it, Belkis, that I have no choice in whether I stay here or have the gate left open for me."

"As if that were possible?" Lallou scoffed. "Where would you go, into the desert where the sun at its zenith would burn that white skin from your bones? Be grateful for the concessions made on your behalf by a man who doesn't have to make them, for as you say, to him you are but a woman and he could keep you in close confinement if he wished. But you will be allowed to go about Beni Zain with your *fatima* in attendance; you will be able to ride with him, pay desert calls on those of the tribe who live in the wilder regions, for Zain is much more civilized than some of the other caids, you know. Belkis and I can expect marriage with such as they, so think yourself fortunate."

"You and Belkis were brought up to this kind of life." Sarah gestured around the apartment, with its tall arching doors, its slim chains to which Moorish lamps were attached, and outside their walled garden with its acorn-shaped arcades, palm trees and exquisite tilework. "Your gilded prison suits you, and you have never dreamed of a knight errant because from small girls you have been taught that men are your masters and your place in life is to please them. It comes hard that I have to learn such a lesson in my twenties, don't you agree?"

Sarah smiled wryly when she said this, for she didn't see how the lesson was ever going to be learned, let alone put to the test. She had no intention of bowing down to Zain Hassan and being the meek and adoring pet at his heels, grateful for any small kindness which he might show her.

"I understand how you feel," Belkis said softly. "Love is a precious flame that can only grow if there are two pairs of lips to breathe it into life and two hearts to cherish it. If it has to burn alone, it can only make the heart ache."

"How very poetic," drawled Làllou, but the look she gave her sister was a shrewd one. "Be sure you got that from a book and not from the lips of a man."

"How could that happen?" Sarah asked, in defence of Belkis. "The *serayi* is too well guarded for that."

"Yes, by guards." Lallou was still staring at the face of Belkis, the lips young and red against the honey skin, like a pair of softly open petals. "Don't do anything foolish, little sister. Think of the mother of Zain – *just think!*"

Sarah's heart gave a jump of apprehension and she found herself looking at the younger sister, with that big-eyed, heart-melting face – half child and half a woman.

"The *kasbah* guards aren't eunuchs," Lallou added, "as they were in the old days. As I told you, Zahra, our brother is not so uncivilized as you persist in thinking him, and when our father died those poor, fat remnants of men were pensioned off and real tribesmen were commissioned into the service of the Khalifa's household, and some of them are very fine specimens of men. Daylis bin Bedari, for instance, could pluck hearts as the gardeners pluck dates from the trees, but for all his fine face and body he is only a poor young man and it wouldn't pay him to cast his flashing eyes above his station. It couldn't get him anything but trouble – you know that, don't you, Belkis?"

Belkis glanced huntedly about and the fear struck Sarah that this pretty young thing might have developed a crush on that good-looking guard; hadn't she noticed herself how very charming he was, and eager to be friendly. As far as she was concerned it would go no further than that, but Belkis had led a secluded life and she was at the age when girls started to have romantic dreams, and the sisters of a Khalifa had no right to such dreams, for they must marry men of his choosing; men of importance to the Beni Zain.

"Come, Belkis, let's go out into the *zariba* and be cool," she urged the younger girl outside, where there was the refreshing sound of a fountain splashing water into its stone basins. The walls of the garden were heavy with flowering vines which had crept up and down and around every available piece of stonework. The effect was lovely, a combination of stunning scents and colours. They wandered among the great boughs of jasmine of white and wine, and on a sudden impulse Sarah took a cloud of the jasmine in her hands and pressed it to her face – a foolish thing to do, for with a startled, angry buzz a great bee flew out of the flowers and aimed its sting at her face. She gave a cry and felt a pain in her lower lip ... Belkis also gave a cry and flew in the direction of a group of chennar trees. A robed figure emerged and Sarah, feeling the spread of the pain and a growing alarm, saw the figure of Raschid bearing down on her.

"You are stung, *sitt*?" He spoke the words in heavily accented English, and Sarah gave him a surprised look. His sun-browned face, with its clipped beard, was bent to her and she saw concern in his black eyes, and she also saw that Belkis was clinging to his arm.

She nodded and the beat of her heart was strangely heavy. "Come!" Without hesitation the guard swung her off her feet into his arms. "We must go at once to the *hakim*!"

Sarah could feel her mouth swelling up even as Raschid marched with her along the corridors of the *kasbah*, Belkis running along behind him in her tiptilted *babouches*. *This is the one,* Sarah thought dimly. *It's Raschid whom she likes.*

In a room off the great hall she was placed on a divan, and now the pain had worsened and the fear had increased. Now she caught the rumble of Arabic and couldn't grasp a word of what was said; all she knew was that the *hakim* was the doctor, and when she felt the trembling clutch of Belkis' hand she tried to smile and found it a torment.

"But it was only a bee ... " She mumbled the words and was horrified by her inability to make the statement clearly. She tried to sit up, but firm hands pressed her back against the cushions, and suddenly all the misery welled up inside her and the frightened tears spilled from her eyes.

"*Zain*," she heard the name and saw in a daze of tears the figure of Belkis running across the room to someone who had just entered. The tears made a shimmering mosaic of that hard brown face and those glittering blue eyes. Sarah saw him coming towards her and he was clad all in black, like a figure of doom. He bent over her and she heard a strange sound in his throat. "By my eyes, what have you done?" he groaned.

Then, a harsh strength back in his voice, he shot an order over his shoulder. The sleeve of her shirt was quickly rolled up, a sharp needle plunged into a vein, and then it seemed to Sarah that every light in the world went out and everything was black. She had a vague impression that she tried to reach out and that she tried to say something . . . they told her afterwards that she fainted from shock and the effect of the powerful injection to offset the sting of the bee, which had plunged directly into her lip and put her in grave danger of being choked as the tissues of her face and neck swelled up.

Sarah came back to awareness in her bed, the filmy netting drawn around her so that she felt protected and hazy and languid all at the same time.

She didn't want to think about her alarming experience, but she couldn't keep her mind from wandering back over the details . . . that gush of jasmine scent seemed as if it was still in her nostrils and her mouth still throbbed . . . she felt afraid of touching her face, but when she did so she found its contours smooth and slim and no longer distorted.

Oh God, she thought, how awful I must have looked . . . no wonder that horrified expression had come into Zain Hassan's eyes and he had made that strange sound in his throat. She must have looked like a gargoyle with her face all swollen up!

At the thought she couldn't control a small groan, and the next instant her *fatima* was at the bedside. After studying Sarah a moment through the netting she drew it aside. "The *sitt* is thirsty?" she softly asked.

Sarah nodded and was helped to sit up so she could sip cool fruit juice through a silver straw. "Why do I feel so weak?" she wanted to know. "Was it the injection they gave me?"

"It had to be strong medicine." The girl stroked the tousled red hair away from Sarah's brow. "The *hakim* say you have good fighting blood."

Sarah smiled slightly, and then winced at the soreness of her swollen lip. She asked for the hand mirror and studied her face in it; her lower lip was decidedly bee-stung, but the rest of her face was back to shape, though she looked awfully pale with shadows under her eyes.

"What a fool thing to do," she murmured. "I took hold of a bunch of flowers and kissed them, but they looked so heavenly – I might have fighting blood, but there doesn't seem to be much of a cure for my impulsiveness. Was the Khalifa fearfully – annoyed?"

"Annoyed, *sitt*?" The young maid looked at her with puzzled eyes. "I hear that he was most worried, for these things can be fatal – as it was seven years ago with his son, the little prince."

A little jolt shook Sarah's heart and once again she recalled that look of horror in the glinting blue eyes. Of course, seeing her like that would have brought back some of the agony of watching his own flesh and blood die of a sting, for in the child's case there had been small hope of saving him. A scorpion had jabbed him straight in a vein, whereas her attacker had been a bee and Raschid had been swift in getting help for her.

Raschid and Belkis . . . oh, there could be no mistaking that look which had passed between them. Sweet Belkis, in love with one of her brother's guards and aware that it was hopeless to dream of belonging to that tall, desert-hard man with the clipped black beard. Somehow Sarah wasn't surprised, for she had sensed herself that there was something quietly chivalrous about the tall, dark Raschid. He would certainly seem a romantic figure to a girl kept in seclusion, with his speckless robes and that curving knife in his belt. How often, Sarah wondered, did the couple meet beneath the chennar trees, and how long could it go on before such meetings became emotionally dangerous?

"Remember Zain's mother," Lallou had said, and Sarah caught her breath at the awful implication in those words.

"You must sleep, *sitt*," her *fatima* said quietly, "and allow the medicine to do its work. Are you quite at ease, my lady?"

"In body," Sarah said, "but my mind keeps going round and round and my thoughts won't give me much peace. Can you sing to me, Analita, as if I were a child again? How quickly we put aside childish things, and how we would go back if we could – into the loving arms."

"I will sing if my lady wishes it, but I have no knowledge of English songs –"

"No, a desert song, Analita, with all that lost in time quality – you know what I mean."

The *fatima* nodded and a faint smile touched her lips. "The *sitt* is a little sad, eh, and yet she should be thankful –"

"Oh, I am! It's for others that I feel – melancholy. If one only had the power to make – to make love the most important thing, with nothing else mattering. Analita, I must be a little lightheaded!"

"Yes, *sitt*." The *fatima* drew the netting with her gentle, coffee-coloured hands, and then she knelt on one of the leather floor cushions and sang as Eastern girls are taught to sing from small infants, one of those strange, wailing songs from out of the distant past when three kings on camel-back followed a star to a stable.

It was infinitely sad and yet soothing and Sarah's lashes

drifted down over her eyes and she began to sink into that velvet limbo where the mind and body could at last relax. But after a few minutes Sarah began to toss and turn and to mutter feverishly to herself. "Gran!" The word rang out. "Oh, Gran, don't leave me! What will I do – what, Gran, be a good girl? Oh yes, I promise to be good!"

And so it went on, that troubled tossing to and fro, and the muttering of phrases that would only have made sense to Sarah herself. Suddenly a frightened look came into the eyes of the *fatima* and she ran from the room and was gone about seven or eight minutes. She didn't return, and in her place came a tall figure in tunic and *sirwal*. He closed the door behind him, came straight to the bedside and drew aside the netting. He stared down a moment at Sarah, and then his lean, strong hands clasped her shoulders and with his lips close to her ear he spoke softly yet firmly.

"You may go home, Zahra. It will be arranged that you leave Beni Zain as soon as you are fit for the journey. Do you hear me, child? You will never again be made to do anything – anything at all that you don't wish to do. *Hilwa*, do you understand me?"

Her eyelids fluttered open, her lashes lifted, and there above her was the one face in all the world that should have increased her unrest. Instead she gazed at him in a sudden stillness, the pale silk of the pillow framing her tousled hair and her shadowed green eyes.

"There, that is what you wanted, eh, to have the gates thrown open for you? They stay open, Zahra, and you may walk through them and ride away whenever you are ready to go."

"The gates of the *kasbah*?" she murmured.

"*Ay*, the gates of your prison. I could give you no better a get-well present, eh?"

Sarah gazed up into his face and the strangest thing of all was that she wanted to reach up her hands and feel the warm skin, the hard bones, the deep chin cleft . . . she wanted their reality against the tips of her fingers, but now he was telling her that she was free to go, and it was more awful than when Gran had died and the little old house at Bow had felt so empty, with no dear, demanding voice to tell her to be a good girl.

A sob for yesterday, and a sob for today broke in Sarah's throat.

"All right," she said huskily. "Whenever you say I must go."

"There is no *must* about it, Zahra. I am giving you what you want, so be pleased and then you will have a good sleep and be rested –"

"It isn't what I want at all," she heard herself say. Then she caught at her underlip with her teeth, gave a quick cry of pain, and the next moment was dragged close to a strong chest and a powerfully beating heart.

"Kissing flowers," he said harshly, even as she felt his lips crushed against her hair. "Why not me, eh? Why not come and kiss me – at least I wouldn't poison you. Is that what you think, that Zain Hassan is poison?"

She could feel him rocking her, like a child, and with a wild wonderment and a longing she pressed her face into his flesh and muscle. Was this what she wanted, after all, this strong, haughty, all-powerful man? To be kissed, hugged, needed . . . ?

"I'm lightheaded," she murmured. "That bee sting has gone to my brain and none of this is real –"

"Do you want this to be real, Zahra?" He drew a fraction away from her and gazed down long and hard into her upraised face. "My sisters told me that you longed only for the gates to be opened so you could leave Beni Zain. You begged for that and said I was too much a tyrant to let you go. I am not quite a tyrant, *hilwa*, though at times I must do things that might strike you as hard, but seeing your little face all swollen up and the pain and

fear in your eyes – as soon as the *hakim* said you were out
of danger I went at once to the mosque and swore on my
knees that I would grant you the thing most dear to your
heart, and surely we both know what that is?"

He looked down deeply into her eyes and again she saw
that dark and haunted look . . . the look she had seen
during the storm when he had spoken of the thunder and
the death of his little boy.

"What is it that I want, grand master?" she asked.

"To leave me," he said simply.

She absorbed the words, took them into her heart and
mind and tested their simplicity . . . their fearful loneliness.

Then she shuddered and her fingernails dug into him as
she clenched him with her hands. "There's nothing to go
back to," she said. "I'm ready to give you what you want."

"What is it that I want, Miss Innocence?"

"A son," she said. "A little boy to replace the one you
lost. That much I believe I can give you."

"Not your heart?" His hand was pressed against her,
warm through the nightdress that was a mere ripple of
apricot silk around her slimness. "I feel it quickly beating
and I'm so hungry for it that I could bite it out of your body
– ah, then it jumped. Why, Zahra? Why does it jump
like that, because I frighten you?"

She shook her head at him wonderingly and felt the
soft, thrilling caress of his fingers. She moved restlessly
closer to him and of their own accord her lips were against
the side of his neck, feeling the warm skin, the tendons,
the beating pulse. "Yes – no – I'm so muddled up. Why
do I feel like this?"

"Do you like it?" His lips travelled down the *décolleté*
of her nightdress. "You are a good girl, Zahra, but you
always seemed afraid to be a warm one."

"No," she whispered, "I was always afraid that in return
for warmth I would only get coldness. When you looked
at me I knew you were remembering Farah. When you

183

looked out into the desert I felt your longing to be with her. You touch me now because I'm a woman in a bed and you are a man—"

"Is that all it is?" He gripped her hair, but not painfully, and held her so she was quite at his mercy. "*Ay*, I loved Farah and I remember her with gentleness and gratitude, but life is ruthless, my *bint*, and I am alive, and the servant and master of my people. The job is a greatly demanding one, and there are days when I would give anything to be able to walk into my own apartment and find there a kind, warm, green-eyed, generous lover, running into my arms and shutting out the cares and sometimes the cruelties. I took you from Casablanca airport and brought you here, hoping it would work. Yes, like some barbarian, as you called me, abducting you — ah, Zahra, how often I have smiled to myself, remembering that first journey together. If only it had been so, that I were only a desert adventurer who could go where I willed with my woman. There in the desert I'd teach you — by Allah, what I'd teach you!"

His eyes flamed, his head came down to her, and it didn't matter that it hurt like hell when his lips captured hers. It was the hungry, aching kiss of a man who wanted her . . . wanted her madly, and her hands found his neck and clung to that warm, smooth column as if it were her lifeline. She melted . . . melted against him, and yes, this really was what she had been searching for, striking so forcibly, so deeply, so that her heart opened and this one person stepped inside . . . mysterious, a little terrifying, and quite wonderful.

His lips drew slowly, reluctantly away from hers and his eyes were smouldering. "Your poor lip — forgive me."

"Hurt me, beat me," she murmured, "I've been such a fool. Shut fast the gates, Zain, keep me here and never let me go."

"Mean it, Zahra," he said roughly. "Don't cry for your freedom after the sword has struck our door seven times,

184

and one by one I undo the hundred pearl buttons of your bridal kaftan, let down your flame coloured hair, and kiss the soles of your slim white feet. You know the words of the Koranic marriage by now."

"Be humble," she kissed his eyes one by one. "Be modest, obedient, and always pleasant to my lord and master. Yes, I know the words, El Zain."

She smiled, and it was then that she thought of Belkis and what she could do for her and her tall Raschid.

"Be Zahra," he whispered, deep in his throat. "Be always my Zahra of the desert fires and the wolfskins."

"With pleasure, my lord!"

She lay there drowsily in his arms, and thought how fast the moon was waxing into the full golden globe that would swing above the alluring sands when she and this man faced the *ma'zoun*, their right hands clasped together as they repeated the marriage vows of Islam. She would then be his *arousa* in masses of veiling reaching to the ground, and he would be hers, proud, tempered, fatalistic man of the desert.

"*Nourmahal,*" he murmured. Light of the harem.

Best Seller Romances

Romances you have loved

Mills & Boon Best Seller Romances are the love stories that have proved particularly popular with our readers. They really are "back by popular demand." These are the six titles to look out for this month.

STRANGE ADVENTURE
by Sara Craven

Young Lacey Vernon was being more or less forced to marry the Greek tycoon Troy Andreakis to save her father from ruin – but as time went on she began to realise, unwillingly, that perhaps she wasn't dreading him as much as she had imagined she was. But that was before she learned what kind of man Troy really was . . .

SWEET PROMISE
by Janet Dailey

Erica Wakefield had met Rafael Torres in Mexico – where their relationship had been brief but dramatic. Now, over a year later in Texas, she had met him again – and he had the power to wreck her whole life. Would he use it?

Mills & Boon

JUNGLE OF DESIRE
by Flora Kidd

It was largely her fault, Diana knew, that her marriage to Jason Clarke had foundered after a few months. Now, in Ecuador, the two of them had met again. In these exotic surroundings, would they be able to rebuild their marriage – or would the new problems of this different life wreck it for ever?

THE UNWILLING BRIDEGROOM
by Roberta Leigh

There was only one word for the method Melisande Godfrey had employed to force André Lubeck into marrying her: blackmail. She had been motivated solely by revenge, and had never paused to think what she would do once he *had* married her; certainly she hadn't expected to fall in love with him. And now, of course, he felt nothing for her but contempt . . .

WILD ENCHANTRESS
by Anne Mather

When young Catherine Fulton arrived in Barbados to spend the next few months under the guardianship of Jared Royal, she was no more enthusiastic about the arrangement than he was – and she went out of her way to give him as bad an impression of her as she could. But she couldn't really disguise the fact that he attracted her now just as much as he had all those years ago . . .

THE BURNING SANDS
by Violet Winspear

Was Sarah doing the wisest thing in accepting a job as companion to the sisters of a Khalifa in the heart of the Moroccan desert? It would seem not – for as soon as she was established there, with no hope of escape, the Khalifa Zain Hassan bin Hamid announced that he had other plans for her . . .

the rose of romance

Best Seller Romances

Next month's best loved romances

Mills & Boon Best Seller Romances are the love stories that have proved particularly popular with our readers. These are the titles to look out for next month.

AVENGING ANGEL Helen Bianchin
A GIFT FOR A LION Sara Craven
FIESTA SAN ANTONIO Janet Dailey
PRINCE FOR SALE Rachel Lindsay
ALIEN WIFE Anne Mather
THE LOVE BATTLE Violet Winspear

Buy them from your usual paperback stockist, or write to: Mills & Boon Reader Service, P.O. Box 236, Thornton Rd, Croydon, Surrey CR9 3RU, England. Readers in South Africa-write to: Mills & Boon Reader Service of Southern Africa, Private Bag X3010, Randburg, 2125.

Mills & Boon
the rose of romance